MIDNIGHT OWL

A Joe Leverette Mystery Book 1

VIV DREWA

Lavish Publishing LLC

First Edition

A Joe Leverette Mystery, Book 1

2021 Lavish Publishing, LLC

All Rights Reserved

Published in the United States by Lavish Publishing, LLC, Midland, TX

Cover Design by: Victor R. Sosa

Cover Images: CANSTOCK

Paperback Edition

ISBN: 9781649000101

www.LavishPublishing.com

Contents

Acknowledgments   vii

Chapter 1   1
Chapter 2   9
Chapter 3   13
Chapter 4   23
Chapter 5   29
Chapter 6   33
Chapter 7   39
Chapter 8   43
Chapter 9   51
Chapter 10   59
Chapter 11   63
Chapter 12   69
Chapter 13   79
Chapter 14   89
Chapter 15   97
Chapter 16   103
Chapter 17   113
Chapter 18   123
Chapter 19   129
Chapter 20   143
Chapter 21   153
Chapter 22   161
Chapter 23   169
Chapter 24   175
Chapter 25   181
Chapter 26   187
Chapter 27   199

About the Author   211
Also by VIV DREWA   213
Also from the Lavish Publishing family   215

The late Carl R. Songalewski Jr.
And
Eric Matthew Edwards Sr.

Acknowledgments

ACKNOWLEDGEMENTS

I would like to thank Dr. Daniel Spits, ME of St. Clair County Michigan for his help with procedures.

I would like to send a special 'Thank You' to authors Aaron Paul Lazar his help.

And also, an extra special 'Thank You' to my fabulous beta readers: Jane Friebaugh, Kayla Lambright, Anne Nelson, Karen Oberlander, and Mira Prabhu for their help.

Chapter One

HEATHER NORTH FELT as if someone were following her for weeks now. The sensation was driving her crazy. She lived in a relatively safe area with a short walk from her parking spot to her apartment, but the feeling was much stronger tonight and it made the walk seem a lot longer.

Behind the large SUV to the left of her car, a figure waited. He watched Heather get her purse and sweater out of her car and lock the door. He watched her look around nervously, checking her surroundings before heading to her apartment.

The one thing Heather really didn't like was the lack of fencing between the parking lot and the small, wooded area next to it. There were just too many trees and a lot of places for someone to hide. Her insecurity tonight made it feel even more ominous. A great horned owl gave off three quick hoots making Heather jump and almost drop what she was carrying. Before she had a chance to step away from her car, a strong arm wrapped around her waist and a damp cloth was clamped tightly over her mouth. She felt herself losing consciences and felt her purse, keys and sweater fall to the ground. Then everything went dark.

Heather awoke, groggy and shivering. She was naked and bound a cold steel table. Her arms and legs were stretched apart. Her heart pounded against her chest like it was going to explode. The room had a nasty, pungent smell, like animals. There was a door off to her right.

Frantically, she looked around and saw that she was in a small dimly lit room. It was empty except for the table she was strapped to and one other smaller table. She stared at the other table. There was saw a small chain and some other things she couldn't make out. Her stomach knotted tighter and tighter. Except for the two tables, the room looked filthy. She noticed cobwebs in one corner and a layer of dust on the shelved. There was a bright light hanging from the ceiling just above her.

There was light under the door and shadows that told her there was someone behind it. The room was so quiet. Even the movement behind the door was silent.

An odd sound pierced the quiet atmosphere. Heather strained to listen. It sounded like a zipper but sh couldn't be sure.

"Who's there?" she called out in a trembling, almost squeaky voice that didn't sound like her own.

The light under the door went out and a squeaking sound echoed through the room. A man stood in the doorway. He was wearing a total-body rain suit, surgical cap and mask. Only his eyes were visible.

"Hello, Heather," he said in a calm voice.

"What do you want? Why are you doing this? Who are you?"

"Now, now. I'm here to take you on an adventure," he said. "One that will allow you to pay for all the misery you've caused to a lot of people. I'm going to make sure you'll never hurt anyone again." He took a syringe and injected it into her neck. She started feeling woozy but not like she was going to pass out.

He turned and reached for something on the table. . She looked up at him, seeing he held four strips of fabric. He began applying one of them to each of her limbs, tightly, like a tourniquet, close to her torso.

The binds hurt. She tried to think of something to say but all that came out was, "Please, please don't hurt me."

"Now, now. This will be nothing compared to the grief and misery you've caused. Six people were hurt, two were even family," he said in his calm voice with just a slight inflection when he said 'family'.

She looked into his eyes and frightened her even more. His lifeless eyes were so dark she felt as if she was falling into them.

Once he finished with the tourniquets, he turned back to the table and picked up a small electrical chain saw.

"This is going to hurt. I won't lie to you," he said with a smile showing through the mask. He started the saw and Heather felt as if she were going to vomit.

"Now just lie still. I'll be done in a second."

He began to cut her left leg with the chainsaw a couple of inches below the tourniquet on her leg.

Heather screamed and thrashed trying to get out of her restraints but to no avail. The pain was excruciating. She started hyperventilating.

"Now just relax. We have four more to go." His calm demeanor terrorized her even more. "We don't want you passing out just yet."

He stopped and waited for her to slow her breathing a little.

"If you breathe too hard, you'll lose blood a lot quicker."

She couldn't speak, , she was in shock. All she could do was to stare at him.

He saw her looking at him with wide-eyed terror. Her mouth moved but nothing came out.

He walked around the foot of the table to her right leg.

"Remember what I said. This is going to hurt." He started the saw and proceeded to cut off the right leg.

Again, she started screaming, wishing she could pass out from the pain. Her bladder and bowels emptied. His cut was quick, but the pain was still agonizing!

"I see we had a little accident," he said, moving the leg away from the excrement on the table. "I'll get to that in a little while."

Heather tried desperately to think. What could she have done so wrong that she deserved this? She wasn't that bad of a person. Sure, she knew she pissed off some people, but she only wanted what was best for her and her kids. Was this monster hired by her ex-husband? Was it her ex-husband? He was a bastard, but he wouldn't do anything like this, would he?

The man checked his work on her right leg, and satisfied, moved toward the head of the table. .

"I'll let you rest for a while. Then we can get back to work," he said and took the severed leg to the other side of the table. She saw him put it in a black trash bag and fasten the top. Then he took the other leg and did the same. He looked at Heather and she could see the smile behind the surgical mask.

"Now, I'll let you pick. Right arm or left arm?"

"Fuck you!" was all she could say in a weak, raspy voice. "Why don't you just cut my head off and be done with it?"

"Oh, that's the encore, my dear. We must get the limbs off first. Since you have no preference, I'll start with this one," he said as he walked to her right arm. He turned on the saw and proceeded to cut off her right arm.

Heather couldn't take the pain anymore. She was sure she was going to pass out this time.

He stopped and shut off the saw. "Maybe I'll let you rest for a minute. You're not looking well."

"Fuck you," she tried to say again. She was getting weaker and colder. Even with the tourniquets, she was losing some blood.

He took her detached right arm and walked over to the

table, carefully, almost reverently, placing it in the bag and tying it shut.

He looked over at Heather and saw she was still awake and that made him happy.

She felt as if she were losing her mind. Is this a dream? A fucking dream? The pain was so real. Heather saw the man coming back to her left side and he had the saw.

"Two to go."

She closed her eyes when she heard the saw and the little energy she had left allowed her one weak scream.

"Now I will put this in its bag, and we can get on with the rest," he said.

He picked up the saw and walked over to her again.

"The fun is just beginning. Aren't you excited?" he sounded genuinely enthusiastic. "Don't think you'll feel much. Maybe get really, cold. Ready?"

Heather shook violently from fear and loss of blood. What the hell could be worse?

"Now, my favorite part," he looked into her eyes and smiled. "Are you ready?"

He picked up the saw and turned it on. "I hope you enjoy it as much as I do," he said and brought it toward her neck.

"No, no, no, please, no, no," she could barely speak. She prayed she'd pass out before he started to cut her neck. The terror worked against this and she laid there, eyes opened wide and mouth trying to scream.

He smiled sweetly and brought down the saw.

"Now, wasn't that the ... what's the saying? 'The cat's meow?'" he laughed hysterically and shut off the saw.

"All done."

He walked to her side and released both tourniquets on her legs at the same time, then her arms.

Blood flowed quickly and Heather's body began to convulse as the remaining blood quickly poured onto the table and squirted the wall. Some dripped down to the floor. He put the saw down on the small table, then he stroked her hair and closed her eyes.

He picked up her head and turned it around in his hands.

"So pretty, but such a bitch," he said and put her head into its trash bag.

Chapter Two

AMY LANG BUNDLED up for her morning walk with her German Shepherd mix, Bud. It was a cold Michigan March, and she couldn't wait for spring. She was grateful for the time change though, since it wasn't quite as dark as it would have been.

The county had made a bike and jogging path near the Black River, on the other side of Strawberry Lane where she lived. This made it much easier to take Bud out, and for her to get some exercise before going in to work. In the summer it was lovely. The trees and bushes were in bloom and the river gently flowed, following the path.

They headed out and Amy looked at the barren trees wishing they still had their leaves. The few pines just weren't enough to make it a pretty walk. Even though she was dressed warmly, she shivered from the cold. But for some reason it didn't really feel like the kind of cold you feel from the weather.

About fifteen yards from her door, Bud started to whimper and pull her toward some dead brush. Amy noticed something black and red poking up through the water's edge, caught in the dead brush along the bank. It was surrounded by pieces of ice that were just starting to melt.

Bud got more agitated the closer they came and pulled even harder. She heard a growl come from deep within his throat.

"It's okay, boy. Let's have a look," Amy said as she let Bud lead her. He started barking and pulling her closer.

"Oh my god!" Amy screamed. The black was a trash bag and the red she saw were the painted toenails that were poking through the top that seemed to come open. She started to shake and back away, trying to pull Bud with her. He resisted but eventually let up.

She was frozen for a moment, trying to understand what she was seeing. Amy's heart was in her throat and with a trembling hand she reached into her coat pocket and pulled out her cell phone.

"Port Huron Police, what is the nature of your emergency?" a calm voice asked.

"I think, I..." Amy didn't know what to say.

"Miss, are you all right?"

"I, I, I think there's a woman's leg," Amy felt like she was going to faint.

"Where are you?"

"Oh my god,"

"Miss?"

"I'm on the bike path off Strawberry Lane," Amy finally said. "I think I'm going to be sick."

"We'll have someone there in a few minutes. Stay on the phone with me until they get there."

"Yeah, yeah," was all Amy said before she vomited. There were a few benches nearby and she went to sit down.

"Are you all right?" The voice asked.

"I think so," Amy said as she sat on the bench keeping Bud close.

"They should be there shortly. Are you in any danger?"

"No. I don't think so. I don't see anyone else out here."

Sirens screamed in the early morning air. In a matter of minutes, a police cruiser turned on Strawberry Lane, driving slowly until the officer spotted Amy.. He shut down the siren and pulled to the curb to park.

"I see her," he said just as another patrol car pulled up.

"I'll hang up with her now," the dispatcher said to the officer.

"Miss, the officer is there now," the voice came over Amy's cell phone.

"Okay. Thank you.".

"I'm Officer Mitchell," the young man said, as the second officer approached and nodded hello. "This is Officer Miller. Can you tell us what happened?"

"I was walking my dog and he got upset. He pulled me over there," Amy said, and with a shaky finger, pointed to the black mass at the shore. "When I got to it, I saw it was a woman's leg."

Miller walked to the bag and shook his head. He looked it over without touching it, or anything around it. Then headed over to Mitchell.

"It's a leg, probably female because the toenails are painted," he said.

"You didn't notice anyone else here?" Mitchell asked Amy.

"No. I never do," Amy said. "I come out every morning around this time to walk Bud and get some exercise before I have to get ready for work."

"Okay," was all Mitchell said. Then he got on his radio to call the chief.

Chapter Three

CHIEF BENNY BILLINGSLEY walked up to Joe Leverette's desk and tossed a folder onto it. It was barely after six o'clock in the morning and Leverette looked up at his chief.

"This is for you, Joe," he said, looking older than his fifty-seven years, a permanent frown etched in the lines of his forehead, eyes tired and droopy, and his pencil thin body looking like it needed a total make over, or just a good meal.

"What's this?" Joe picked up the folder and opened it. He let out a long whistle after reading the single page. "So, we have a body dump?"

"No. We have a piece-of-a-body dump," Billingsley said and sat in the chair next to Leverette's desk. "Only a left leg, and it's female according to the intake form."

"You can tell it's female?"

Billingsley ignored his sarcasm. "We just got the call

and I want you and Marsden to head out. Two patrol officers are out there now with the woman who found it, Mitchell and Miller. The toenails are painted so we figured it was female. Only the ankle and toes are visible."

"Now-a-days that doesn't mean much," Leverette said as he glanced at the page. "Could be a cross dresser. We'll head straight out. Doc on his way?"

"Yeah, and the crime unit," Billingsley said, rubbing his temples.

Phil Marsden walked up to his desk across from Leverette's, slowing his pace when he saw the chief there. Marsden was not a fan of the chief, though he respected his position.

"Hi Chief," Marsden said, trying to sound professional.

"Hi. Got a case for the two of you. Leverette will go over everything on the way to the scene."

Billingsley got up and walked back to his office.

"Must be a hell of a case for the chief to come and talk to you," Marsden said. "What's it about?"

"Grab your coat and I'll fill you in. There's not too much yet."

They got to their assigned car and Leverette handed Marsden the file. He let him look at it before he started telling him what the chief said.

"Damn. Just a leg?" Marsden hated these cases. He didn't have trouble dealing with shootings or stabbings, but he couldn't stand dismembered bodies, or trips to the morgue when the doc was working on a corpse.

"Yup. Two cops are there with the woman who found it," Leverette said. He didn't turn on the lights or sirens. It was a short drive from the Port Huron Police Department, and he didn't want to alarm the neighborhood just yet, though he figured the first officer's sirens probably already did that. They turned in to the area off Strawberry Lane and parked near the other squad cars. As they got out of the car, Leverette studied the area. There was a path joggers or bikers could use near the Black River; across the street there were nice homes. The path had some lights. Dead trees and shrubs were scattered about but offered little, if any, privacy for a dump. He wondered how long ago the leg had been put in the river. He knew with the ice still present, it hadn't been dumped here but had flowed here from somewhere farther upstream.

Leverette and Marsden walked over to the officers and Amy.

"We're waiting for the crime unit to get here, but we didn't see anything other than the bag with part of the leg poking through," Officer Miller said. A small group of people were starting to gather around.

"Better tape off the area before too many people show up," Leverette said to Miller.

"Was just about to do that," Miller said, and he and Mitchell headed to one of the cars and got out the tape. They decided on a perimeter and Miller took one end of the tape and attached it to a tree near the bank. Mitchell took the spool and brought it around and tied it to a strong shrub, leaving a good sized area inside the tape. When they were finished, they walked back to Leverette and Marsden.

Marsden, an obvious lady's man, turned to Amy.

"Hi, I'm Detective Phil Marsden, this is my partner Detective Joe Leverette. We would like to ask you a few questions."

Amy, a petite blond with big brown eyes that were filled with tears, managed a smile.

"Sure. But I already told them what happened."

"I know. Why don't we go over to the car and have a chat?" Marsden wanted to put a good distance between himself and the leg.

Leverette didn't mind. He hated talking to witnesses. Victims were all right, though, or murderers, or thieves, or any criminal. He knew Marsden had the 'gift' as the chief called it, to talk to witnesses.

Marsden's dark curly hair and blue eyes seemed to be just what some people needed to regain their composure. Not to mention his gentle voice.

He followed Marsden and Amy to the car.

"What time were you walking here?" Marsden asked.

"I always bring Bud out before work, just after six am. We go the same path every day," she said.

"How long have you been doing this?"

"Five years now," she said, and her eyes started to tear up again. "It was nice when they put the path and lights in. That poor woman."

"What made you notice it?"

Amy tensed at the intensity of his voice. "We were just walking, and Bud got upset and pulled me toward it. I saw the black bag and something red. When I got closer, I saw it had a tear in it and then I saw the toes." This made her eyes tear up even more. "My god!"

The crime scene team got there and started looking around and collecting samples. Leverette didn't have the patience for this kind of work, even though he'd scan the area for things that didn't look like they belonged there.

A van pulled up and parked next to Leverette's car. The M.E. had arrived and with much effort, managed to work his way out of the van. Dr. George Carrington had been the County M.E. for close to forty years. He was bald, tall, and obese. He waddled over to the detectives.

"We have a leg," he said. "Did they find any more of her?"

"Not so far. The dive team is just getting suited up to check the river. They haven't found anything else near shore," Leverette told him. "I don't know how they can get in that water in this cold."

Dr. Carrington just laughed. "I guess they're used to it. Especially after this horribly cold winter." He waddled over to examine the leg.

The dive team went in with poles and started to gently run them on the bottom, then went farther in until they were out of sight. Their flashlights were visible for a few seconds then they too disappeared.

Marsden had his arm around Amy and was still asking her questions.

"I don't understand how else I can help," she said, looking up at his six-foot frame.

"You'd be surprised at how even the smallest things could be a big help," he gently told her.

She thought for a minute, but nothing came to mind. "Sorry, I just don't know."

"Well," he reached into his pocket and pulled out a card. "If you think of anything, and I mean anything, call me."

"Okay, I will" she said, as she tried to compose herself for the walk home.

"Was she able to tell us anything more?" Leverette asked as he and Marsden watched Dr. Carrington examine the leg.

"No. Didn't see anything or hear anything. Once she calms down a bit, she might think of something to tell us," Marsden said. "I get the feeling she's not telling me something."

Marsden looked at his partner and pictured him on an old ship, Schooners, he thinks they were called. Leverette looked so much like the sailors back then, with his silver/black hair and long sideburns that connected at his chin. Leverette's eyes were even a cold, steel gray. He was thin like Marsden, but about two inches shorter.

Dr. Carrington slowly made his way over to the two detectives huffing and puffing. He stopped for a minute before he spoke.

"It's a female leg," he said once he got his breath back. "Looks like it was taken off by some type of professional. Unfortunately, the poor thing was still awake when it was taken off."

"Killer or doctor?" Leverette asked.

"Either. I'll know more once I check her out at the morgue," Dr. Carrington waited for either of the detectives to say something, and when they didn't, he turned to leave.

One of the cops brought the leg and put it in the back of his van. The doctor squeezed himself behind the wheel, shut the door and left.

The two divers came out of the water shaking their heads. No other body parts were found, just an old bike, three tires, and some tools. The divers couldn't go too much farther because of the strong cross current.

"Looks like they're done, and the crime scene group is still going through the shrubs. We might as well go and wait for the doc's report," Leverette said. "I'll send the patrol guys to check out the homes across the street. The crime guys, er people, are going to check the water's edge for several miles to see if more bags floated down."

Leverette went over to the two officers and told them what he wanted them to do. They said they would get back to him once they had finished.

Marsden was bothered by what Amy wasn't telling him. He wondered if she saw something and was too scared to say anything or if she was part of it. She didn't seem like the kind of person who would steal a pen from her place of employment. But she could just be a good actress.

The ride back to the station was quiet. Leverette always drove since he was the senior of the two, by about sixteen years. Marsden didn't care today because it gave him time to think. And since Leverette wasn't much of a conversationalist the quiet, though appreciated, was uncomfortable.

"What's up?" Leverette asked, the silence bothering him.

Marsden just looked out his window.

"I've never seen you this quiet."

"It just feels like she's hiding something," Marsden said not looking at Leverette.

Amy Lang got back to her home and let Bud off his leash then fed and watered him. The coffee was ready, so she poured a cup and sat at her kitchen table.

She worried that the one detective, Marsden, thought she was hiding something from him. She could tell by the way he looked at her. Amy wasn't even sure if she was. If she told him she had a dream about that leg he'd think she was crazy. She was beginning to wonder if she was.

The leg was found close to her home and that could mean she put it there. But if they checked her home, they wouldn't find anything to incriminate her.

The water hadn't been moving much because of the ice that still covered some of the river. That was probably what tore the plastic bag. Why did she have to find it?

Why did she have that stupid dream? Should she tell someone?

She took a sip of her coffee and went over the dream in her mind. It was so grisly. She could smell the blood and a rancid odor. She felt the cold of the room he was working in. Amy saw the body of the woman lying on a table with her arms, legs and head cut from her torso. She watched him put the pieces in the black plastic bags and tie each one off. The torso was another story. He had to put one bag over one end and cover the other with another bag. Then he used a rope to secure it in the center. It would have fit in just one bag, but this was better in his eyes.

Amy watched in horror and then the man looked up and right into her eyes and pressed a finger to his lips making a 'shh' sound.

This had made her wake with a start. She was shaking and sweating and couldn't fall back asleep.

Now she looked at the clock and it was midnight. Outside, an owl gave off three quick hoots sounding almost like a warning. It sent a shiver through Amy's body and she looked around for Bud. He was curled up on the bed next to her and looked up tilting his head wondering what was going on.

"Just had a bad dream, Bud," she said.

Her phone rang and made her jump out of her chair. She spilled her coffee on the table and her jogging outfit. Amy was glad she had the day off. That dream and the leg she found left her frazzled.

"Hello," she answered, her body still trembling.

"Ms. Lang, this is Detective Marsden, we were wondering if you could come down to the station for a few more questions."

"I don't know what else I can tell you," she said, feeling his suspicion of her. "Okay. I can be there in an hour."

"Fine, see you then," Marsden said and hung up.

Chapter Four

"NOW, what in the hell do you think she could be hiding?" Leverette asked shaking his head. "That poor thing was so terrified. She didn't act like she was hiding anything. Hell, she doesn't look like she has it in her to do something like this."

"I don't know, I don't know," Marsden said. "She might have just seen something and is afraid to say anything. Maybe she'd been threatened."

"You're reaching," Leverette said. He looked up and the chief waved them to come into his office. "Chief wants us."

Marsden didn't want to go but knew better. The two got up and went into the chief's office.

"You two are going to be very busy," Billingsley said and picked up three more files. "Three more parts. Right leg and two arms."

"Shit. Where?" Marsden asked.

"The leg in a sewer drain in Fort Gratiot, right arm in a factory lot in the industrial area, and the left arm in an abandoned home in Port Huron," Billingsley said and handed the files to Leverette.

"Same lady?" Leverette asked.

"Same nail polish according to the primaries, even on the fingers. Testing showed this is the same woman. I'm waiting on DNA to see if we can identify her."

"So, we're just missing the head and torso," Leverette said as more of an afterthought.

"Haven't gotten anything from Dr. Carrington yet, so we don't know if she's in the system."

"I'll checked for missing persons. At least we have the fingerprints from the hand. And we do have sixteen missing women," Marsden said.

"Is anyone at the other locations yet?" Leverette asked.

"Yeah, some patrol officers. Waiting on Carrington and the others," Billingsley said. "I'm not sure where anyone is going to first, so you might want to call."

"Have to call Amy Lang first," Marsden said. "She's supposed to meet us here in about half an hour."

Leverette looked at his partner. "I'll call her."

Marsden looked at him. "Just be nice."

"Don't forget about Carrington," Billingsley said.

"Will do," Marsden said and headed to his desk. He picked up the phone and called Carrington.

"He already left," a voice on the other end said.

"Did he say where he was going?" Marsden asked.

"No, but two of his associates will be going to each of the other ones."

"Okay, thanks," Marsden said and hung up.

Leverette was just walking to his desk when Marsden hung up.

"Where to first?"

"Doesn't matter, Carrington and two of his people have headed out to each of the locations," Marsden said. "So, it doesn't matter. Work our way back?"

"Yeah, that sounds good," Leverette said and handed the files to Marsden as they left the squad room.

In the car, Marsden looked through the three files that contained the intake sheets. "Wow. The parts are spread around but not that far from each other. The sheriff's department will probably be there."

"No doubt," Leverette said as he turned on Simpson, off of Pine Grove and headed to the end of the street.

"Look at that," Leverette said as he pulled over to park. "He didn't even try to hide this one."

Marsden got out and crunched up his face. The leg was just lying over the drain wrapped in the same type of black trash bag. A man was standing with the officers. They were all shaking their heads.

"They're keeping this out of the press?" Marsden whispered the question as he and Leverette walked over.

"Yeah, for now. Once we find all the parts and can

identify her body, Billingsley might let it out. Depends on what we find."

Kenneth Denton was the man who found the leg and he seemed pretty upset over it. He was giving his statement to the officers who were there when Leverette and Marsden walked up.

"I didn't know what it was until I went to pick it up," Denton was saying. "It felt weird, so I thought I'd call you."

"Did you touch the bag?" Leverette asked.

"Yeah, but I have my mittens on," Denton said and showed Leverette his hands.

"What brought you down here today?" Leverette asked.

"I like to jog down this way. It's quiet," he said and turned to look at the two detectives.

"Do you live around here?" Marsden asked looking at Denton's running shoes. They were well-worn.

"Not far. I'm in the apartment building on Krafft Road. Not far from here," he pointed to the apartments.

"This is a regular routine then?" Marsden asked.

"Yeah. Every day, rain, snow, or shine. I had a mild heart attack two years ago and my doctor said it would be all right to go a short distance and this is perfect. Or, was until today."

"Did you see anything out of the ordinary when you got here?" Marsden took over the questioning.

"No, just that bag," Denton said and shook his head. "Why would someone do something like that?"

Marsden just shook his head. He looked Denton directly in the eye. "And you're sure you didn't see anything?"

"No. I never do. That's why I like it," Denton told him. "There's little or no traffic. I have my cell phone if I need help. It's the one with the emergency buttons."

Leverette noticed a few old houses on the other side of the street.

"Have you ever seen any of the people come out while you were here?" Leverette asked.

"The third house. The guy there leaves for work, I think, just as I get here."

"What time was that?" Leverette asked.

"Around 7am. Other than that, nobody."

"Here's my card if you think of anything," Leverette said. "We might call you to come down to the station later. Sometimes things come to you once you calm down from something like this."

"I don't have to be to work until 3pm so I could stop by before that, or we'd have to wait until tomorrow."

"No problem."

Marsden had the same feeling about Denton that he did with Amy. "He knows something, too", he thought.

Leverette noticed the look on Marsden's face. "What now?"

"He knows something," Marsden said as they walked toward the bag.

"What are you? A psychic or something?" Leverette sounded more amused than pissed.

"No. Just a feeling I got when I looked into his eyes," Marsden said, defending himself. "Just like I did with Amy."

"Well, let's head to that house. You got the address?" Leverette asked shaking his head at Marsden.

"Yeah,"

Chapter Five

KEN DENTON AND HIS WIFE, Sarah, lived in a two-bedroom apartment. After their two sons moved out, they decided to sell the house and move into the apartment. After all, they really didn't need the room anymore.

Sarah worked for a family-owned restaurant doing their books and taxes. There were three restaurants in the county, and she handled all three.

Since Ken's heart attack, he had to take a pay cut. He wasn't able to lift the fifty plus pound cartons of plastic parts his factory made anymore. They did offer him a place in their shipping and receiving where a forklift would do the heavier work, and the younger people could lug around the heavier cartons. Ken usually handled the phones and paperwork.

His wife was already at work when he got back from his jog. Ken didn't like the way the one detective looked at him. He was holding back the dream he had the night before, and thought if he said anything the one detective, Marsden, would think he was off his rocker.

He took his sneakers and jacket off in the small coat room. After finding the leg, the memory of that damn dream was coming back. He wished his wife were home.

Ken decided to shave and then take a nice warm shower and get ready for the day. He still had plenty of time before leaving for work and figured the shower would get the chill out of his bones.

The warmth was great, and he felt himself relax a little.

As hard as it was not to think about that dream, it crept up in his mind anyway.

He saw the woman, cut into pieces, lying on a large steel table. Her face covered by her long black hair made it difficult to see who she was. Maybe it was better he couldn't see her. What if he knew her?

The man in the dream picked up her right leg and examined his work. He ran his fingers over the brightly red-painted toenails. Ken saw him smile through the surgical mask he was wearing. Then he heard an owl give out a quick hoot three times. At that point, the man looked right into Ken's eyes and placed his finger to his lips and said "Shh."

Ken had shot up in bed and scared his wife.

"What's wrong?" she'd asked wondering if he was having another heart attack.

He sat there for a minute. "Nothing, just a bad dream."

"You're soaking wet! Want to talk about it?" Sarah

asked. She wondered if he should have stayed off work the entire three months the doctor recommended instead of going back as early as he did.

"No, no," Ken said and got up to go get some water. "Go back to sleep. I'm fine. I'm going to put on fresh pajamas, and I'll be back in bed."

"You sure?"

"Yes. Just going to get some water and change."

Now, even standing in the warm shower Ken's body started to shiver. Those eyes were the darkest he had ever seen. Almost hypnotic. He didn't remember ever seeing eyes like those. They had to have been part of the dream. Or did they? Now he knew the leg was real, but those eyes? He began to shiver much harder and decided to finish his shower and dress in something warm.

Ken made himself a sandwich and sat at the kitchen table. He really wished he weren't alone right now.

As he ate, he went over everything from the morning. Nothing out of the ordinary came to mind. Just the one guy leaving for work as he always did. There were no other people out and no vehicles he didn't recognize. He didn't hear anything, either, or smell anything.

He hoped the cops didn't make him feel nervous with their questions, because he didn't know anything. He'd seen on TV the good cop bad, cop routine and wondered if they really operated like that.

Ken felt sorry for whomever that leg belonged to. He seriously considered changing his jogging path.

Chapter Six

CAROLE SAGE SAT at her kitchen table reading a book and sipped a strong hot cup of coffee. She liked extra cream and sugar in it and her friend, Karen, would tease her about it.

Her cat, Oscar, sat on his perch by the window preening himself. Something blew in front of the window and got his attention. He watched for a second then went back to preening. She loved how his short black hair gleamed in the spring sun.

She hoped the snow would finally be gone. It was a long, cold winter and she was so ready for spring.

Carole, a petite woman with shoulder length light brown hair and hazel eyes, smiled at Oscar and went back to reading. She had the week off and wanted to relax.

"Just like you like your men. Strong, sweet and creamy," Karen would tease about her taste in coffee. Karen was a model-gorgeous brunette with long brown hair, smooth chocolate skin and big brown eyes. She worked as a computer programmer and was at the top of her profession.

When they both started college in 1972, computers were just beginning. One unit took up an entire room at that time, and now you could put them in your pocket. How times had changed.

Carole and Karen both graduated with master's degrees at a time when jobs were easy to find. They'd both been with their perspective companies ever since.

Karen had traveled to Italy and Germany on company business on several occasions and had come back with stories about the men she met. Two years later, she married a fellow she'd met in college. Carole had always thought she would find someone in one of the countries she visited to help with programming problems.

"Quit," was all Carole would say to her friends when they tried to set her up with someone. She was not interested in lasting relationships; her work was her world. She liked it that way.

Carole worked as a chemical analyst at the sugar beet plant in Croswell. She was responsible for the chemical analysis and product quality control systems. She enjoyed her work and did it well.

The only thing she didn't like about this 'gift', was knowing when people were going to die. No matter how hard she tried to ignore the signs they always haunted her. What was she going to do with it anyway? She didn't want it and didn't like it. And, unfortunately, that was all her gift was, knowing when people would die. Her mother, on the other hand, could tell when something was going to happen; good or bad.

She wouldn't admit it to anyone, even though her family and Karen knew, but the real reason she didn't want to get involved with anyone was because she saw her fiancée's death. The vision upset her and when the car crash actually happened, she was devastated.

Brent and Carole had dated for almost two years before he proposed. They set a date and had started making all the arrangements when the accident happened. From that time on she decided she wouldn't get involved with anyone. She didn't want to feel that pain ever again.

She'd returned to her reading when that feeling came over her, the one she'd get when someone would die. Only this time it was different. Generally, she would see the person in her mind's eye and get a weird feeling that caused her to shiver. This time she got the feeling but nothing else. She couldn't put her finger on it, and no person popped in her head.

Carole took a sip of her coffee and tried to figure out what she was feeling. She never had to try to see the person. Their face would be there just after the feeling. Nothing was coming to her. It was really starting to bother her. The only other times it happened like this was when her parents died and she figured it was because they were so close. Was it another relative? Her sister or brother? They'd be at work and someone would have called her.

What was she going to do? She decided to just ignore it and started reading her book again.

The feeling started tugging at her even stronger. She didn't know what to do. In frustration, Carole closed the book so hard it made Oscar jump.

"Sorry, baby. Mama's just having a bad day," she said and smiled at him.

He glared at her for a second then slowly closed his eyes and went back to his nap.

Carole wished she knew someone with her 'gift'. She could check it out on the internet, but she didn't know what to call it. Karen thought she was a sensitive, so she got up to go to her desk where the laptop was sitting.

In the back of her mind she didn't think she really wanted to know. She turned on her laptop and typed 'sensitive' in the search bar.

Look at all the sites! She didn't know where to start. She decided from the top would be best.

Not only did she find articles on sensitive, which is known as HSP, highly sensitive person, but there were books and tests to see if, or how, sensitive someone was. She didn't need the test. Carole decided to just read the articles.

She was fascinated by the information. Actual scientists found this trait to be in everything from bugs to primates as a type of survival strategy, where observation is critical before reacting to a situation.

As for humans, it is believed that about twenty percent have HSP. Their brains are more apt to process information and think about it more deeply than the other eighty percent of the population.

The more overstimulated the HSP, the more it will take notice of situations than others without it.

Carole sat back in her chair and didn't know if she could believe how common this was. She knew not to believe everything on the internet, but some articles were written by professionals.

She went on to find information on spirit mediums who actually spoke to spirits. Carole never spoke to them so she thought she fell somewhere in between.

That feeling pinged in her head again. She didn't recognize the woman she saw but, for the very first time, felt her physical pain. The woman's whole body ached, and Carole felt her fear. It was strong, the fear. Overwhelming. Carole couldn't stand this feeling and wished it away. It didn't leave her. It was worse than having an albatross gripping her shoulders. She thought she would faint.

Carol broke out in a cold sweat and started shaking. She felt as if she were this woman. Then, as quickly as it came, it was gone.

She didn't realize that she was leaning over her coffee cup that was on the kitchen table. When did she get back to the table from her desk? She tried but couldn't remember. Her body had been so tense during this feeling that it ached when she went to sit up in her chair.

Carole looked at Oscar, who was still on his perch. He glared at her and sensed something was wrong. He stood, stretched and jumped down, then walked over to her. He jumped into her lap and started to purr, head-bumping her chin.

"Mama's all right," Carol said and petted him. She was glad this didn't happen when she was working. Not this one, anyway. She had other feelings come to her at work and was able to keep them to herself. This one would have been hard to hide from anyone.

She just wondered what it all meant and hoped it wouldn't come back. She never had one like this. This one had her confused. It really scared her.

Chapter Seven

"JUST GOT A CALL FROM THE LAB," Billingsley said as he walked up to Leverette and Marsden. They decided to stop at the office before heading to the other locations. "It'll take two days or more to get the DNA. Maybe longer if the lab's busy," he looked directly at Leverette.

"We didn't get a look at the other leg so I don't know if the nails were painted," Leverette said, a little disappointed. "Can't you put a rush on it?"

"I'll give them a call and have a uniform drive it over," Billingsley said. "Now we have a right and left leg. You go check out the arms."

"Arms?" Marsden said. "This asshole is putting her all around the county! So, what about the body and head?"

"Not sure how much he carved up the torso," Leverette said. "Barb was at the last scene so we don't know where Carrington will be."

"So, there's a chance the head and body will still be together?" Marsden asked not really wanting to know the answer.

"No telling how much more he did," Billingsley said looking at Marsden now. "He might have just cut off the head, but he could have also cut the torso into pieces."

Marsden's stomach started feeling queasy.

"Hear anything from Carrington yet?" Billingsley asked.

"No. He went to one of the other locations, so we won't get much yet. Barb was heading back to the lab with the other leg," Leverette said. "They're wondering if they'll find the whole body today.We might even get the whole body before lunch."

Marsden felt like he was as white as a ghost.

Leverette noticed and shook his head.

"Well, one arm was found in a factory area and the other at a home," Billingsley said. "You may be right. The rest of her body might be found today."

Marsden had to walk away at this point. He just couldn't take any more of the conversation. If he just didn't picture what they were saying he'd be fine, but unfortunately, he was a visual thinker.

Leverette and Billingsley just looked at each other and chuckled.

"Poor guy," Leverette said. "He's fine when we go to the morgue and Doc doesn't have someone open on the table."

Billingsley just raised his eyebrows. "Well, he's a good detective regardless."

"Once he gets himself together, we'll head out to the other two," Leverette said glancing at Marsden, who was looking out the window at the front of the precinct.

Chapter Eight

LEVERETTE WALKED UP TO MARSDEN.

"You ready?" he asked.

"Yeah, I guess," Marsden answered. "I'm glad we don't get many dismemberment cases."

"I know," Leverette said and honestly felt sorry for the young detective. "Come on, let's get to the factory."

Marsden closed his eyes and sighed deeply. "I'm ready."

They headed out the door and into their car. Marsden pulled the page from the folder to see which factory to go to.

"It's on 24th near Dove," Marsden said as Leverette pulled out the parking lot.

"Not sure if Carrington will be there. Barb wasn't sure which one he went to when I asked her. He and Marcie headed out at the same time she did."

Leverette winced when Marsden said Marcie. He really didn't like her.

"Doesn't matter. He has a good team," Leverestte said as they turned onto Lapeer and headed for 24th.

"Did it say which factory?"

"Parker's Plastics," Marsden answered. "It's in the Industrial Park."

They turned left onto 24th and headed to Dove. Rotating lights from the patrol car led them right to the spot. They pulled into the parking lot and saw that Carrington was examining the arm. He didn't notice them pull in and get out of their car.

The patrol officers had already put a crime scene tape around the area.

"I'll go talk to the patrol guys. That must be the guy who found the arm with them," Marsden said as he got out of the car.

"I'll go see Carrington," Leverette said and headed toward the doctor.

The arm was sitting on top of a pile of pallets. That made it easier for Carrington to look it over.

"Hey, Doc," Leverette said as he approached him.

Carrington, who was slightly leaning over the arm, jumped a little and turned to see Leverette. "Hi," was all he said as he gained his composure.

"Think it's from the same gal?" Leverette asked as he looked at the right arm.

"Nails are painted the same red, and the cut looks the

same. I think it might be. Won't know for sure," he said as he straightened himself.

"I heard they found another arm at a home," Leverette said.

"Yeah, Marcie's at that one. Barb called just now and said she's pretty sure it's the same woman. The other leg, that is."

"I wonder how much more he cut up," Leverette said.

"I was wondering the same thing," Carrington said. "He might have removed the head and cut the body into pieces. Won't know until, or if, we get the rest of her."

"Damn. This case is keeping us busy. We have a criminologist trying to figure it out. Nothing seems to fit a pattern."

"This crazed killer might not follow a pattern," Carrington said. "There have been cases where there is no rhyme-or-reason."

"True," Leverette said. "I'm going to see what Marsden found out." He headed to the four who were near the patrol car. He pulled Marsden away from the group.

"What'd doc say?" Marsden asked.

"He thinks it's probably the same woman," Leverette said. "Won't know for sure until he checks them all."

"Wonder if Gordon found a connection to the dump sites," Marsden said. "He's our best criminologist."

"That would really help. So far, we found parts at the river, by a small street, by this factory and at a house," Leverette said with a look of being in deep thought on his face. "I have no idea."

"The guy who found it is DeShawn Davis. He came in a little while ago," Marsden said. He looked at his watch. It's 7:30 AM. They walked up to DeShawn and the patrol officers.

Leverette had to look up to make eye contact with DeShawn. He had to be close to seven feet tall and had a muscular build on him that would make any bodybuilder jealous. DeShawn was a dark chocolate brown and his shaved head had sweat running down it as though he'd run a marathon. Leverette didn't think he would be afraid of anything.

Marsden, who also had to look up to DeShawn, made the introductions.

"Can you tell us what happened?"

"Like I told the officer, I came out to get some pallets and it was there. Scared the bejesus out of me and I don't scare easily," DeShawn told them.

"What time was it, you found the arm?" Leverette asked.

"Just after seven. I came out to get some pallets and it was there. Well, I saw the black bag and when I picked it up it felt funny. I put it back. I'll give you my prints if you want."

"What about your boss? Did he touch it?" Leverette asked.

"Yeah, but he had gloves with him and put them on first," DeShawn said. "Can I see the arm?"

Marsden was visibly shaken. "You want to see it?"

"Yeah. I wanted to be an ME but didn't have the opportunity to go to school."

"No. Its better you don't," Leverette said. "Dr. Carrington's going to take it to the lab and start running tests."

"Okay," he said, disappointed. He looked at Marsden. "Man, you look like you're about to faint."

Leverette choked back a laugh. "He doesn't like body parts," was all he said.

"Oh," DeShawn said. "You guys still need me? I wanna get back to work and try to put this behind me."

Leverette looked at the cameras on the building.

"Before you go, can you tell me if those cameras work?"

"Yeah. They run twenty-four seven. If you go to the office, they can run you a copy," DeShawn said.

"You can go. We have your information if we need you. And you have ours if you think of anything," Leverette said.

DeShawn and his boss headed back into the factory. Fortunately, they had other pallets they could use and left those alone.

But as DeShawn started getting the other pallets, the dream came back to him. He'd been hoping it would go away. He never remembered his dreams for more than a minute when he woke up. Long enough to laugh at them or try to understand them. This one was hanging on.

He sat down and the dream played in his head. He

remembered seeing a woman's body on a metal-looking table, a man dressed in some kind of plastic outfit with his head and face covered. All DeShawn could see were his eyes. Dark scary eyes. He watched the man put the arm in the black bag and tie off the top.

DeShawn heard three quick hoots from an owl and the man looked him in the eyes. He put his finger to his lips and DeShawn heard him say, "Shh."

Remembering the dream made him shiver. He knew not to say anything to the cops because he didn't believe it was anything more than a bad dream, a dream that wouldn't leave him, but a dream none the less.

Carrington carried the arm to his van and set it in the back. After he shut the doors, he waddled over to Leverette.

"He was really interested in the arm," Leverette told Carrington. "Said he wanted to be an ME at one time."

"That explains why he was trying so hard to get a look at what I was doing while the officers questioned him," Carrington said.

"Nothing personal, Doc, but your job is just ..." Marsden couldn't think of the right words to say and shook his head.

Carrington smiled. "I know. Well, I'm going to the lab. Once Marcie gets back, we'll give her a good looking over," Carrington said and waddled to his van, squeezed in and left.

Leverette noticed Marsden wasn't looking any better.

"Let's head out to the house and then we'll get back to the precinct," Leverette said.

Marsden nodded and followed him to the car. He was worried that he might vomit if he tried to talk.

Chapter Nine

LEVERETTE AND MARSDEN get into their car and Marsden opened the next file.

"The next stop is on White Street near 13th Street," Marsden said. "If I remember right, it's just off Griswold."

"Yeah, I think I have an idea where it is," Leverette said and turned onto 24th toward Griswold.

They rode the rest of the way in silence. Marsden hoped Leverette wouldn't start to tease him. He didn't know why this bothered him when he'd seen bodies mutilated beyond recognition. There was just something about bodies being deliberately cut apart that got to him. He wondered how Leverette did it. He never showed any feelings one way or the other. Not that he was a stone-faced person, he had a smile that made the ladies melt, but he would never show any kind of emotion at a crime scene.

Traffic was moving at a decent pace and they managed

to get there in ten minutes. The patrol car was parked in the driveway, and Marcie was carrying the arm out to her van which was parked in front of the house.

One of the patrol officers was talking with an Asian man who looked terrified. He was sweating and shaking almost uncontrollably. They got out of the car and walked toward them.

The patrol officer saw them and nodded. The young man turned toward them. Leverette figured him to be in his fifties, but he was never good at guessing ages.

"This is Shin Yoo," the officer said. "These are Detectives Leverette and Marsden."

The young man looked at them and tried to smile.

"You own this house?" Leverette asked.

"It was my parents'. My mother passed four years ago, and my father last week," Shin said.

"Sorry for your loss," Marsden said in his calm voice. "Has anyone been living here since?"

"No, my wife and I live in Fort Gratiot. My sister and her husband are in Mount Clemens. We were going to get together to clean out the house and get ready to sell it."

"Why did you come here alone today?" Leverette asked.

This made Shin even more nervous. He wasn't sure how to answer.

"I was just checking to be sure nobody broke in. The neighbors have been keeping an eye on it, but they can't watch it all the time,"

"Where did you find the arm?" Leverette asked a little

gruffer than he meant to. He thought about apologizing but decided not to.

Shin's eyes grew wide. "I didn't put it there!" he said defensively. "I found it in the kitchen sink."

"I wasn't accusing you. I'm sorry," Leverette said.

"I'm sorry, too," Shin said. He realized everyone was on edge, not just him.

Leverette looked at his watch. It was just about 8:30AM.

"Were you on your way to work?" Leverette asked.

"I have the week off and thought I'd stop by. I was even thinking about doing a little cleaning," Shin said.

"What do you do?" Marsden asked.

"I'm an independent programmer. I build firewalls and maintain them." He thought about telling them about the dream he had last night but then thought better of it. They might think he was crazy, or they'd think he did this and was trying to use an insanity defense.

Marsden picked up on Shin's hesitation, just like he had with Amy and Denton. All three of them were hiding something. Might be a good idea to get them to the precinct and have a chat.

He handed Shin his card.

"If you think of anything, please call. Or if you know of someone who saw something and they don't want to talk to us," Marsden said. "We might call you to come in to talk with us."

"Sure. No problem," Shin said, taking the card.

"You can go now," Leverette said.

"Okay. I want to call my sister and let her know what's going on," Shin said.

"You won't be able to get into the house for a while," Marsden said. "We'll have a team go in to give it a look-over. I'll let you know when it'll be all right for you to finish what you need to do."

Shin just nodded and walked to his car and drove away.

Marcie saw Leverette and waved. Marcie had a huge crush on him even though he was twenty-three years her senior, and everyone knew it. Marsden thought it was funny to see her act like a schoolgirl around Leverette and would tease him about it. But today was different, he didn't feel like teasing or being teased. This case really bothered him.

Marcie closed the back of the van and headed toward them in a girly sway. Leverette stiffened, wishing she'd just go back to the lab.

"Hiya, Detective," she said in a sing-song voice, looking directly at Leverette.

"Hello," Marsden said.

Leverette forced a smile.

"Quite a case, huh?" she asked still looking directly at Leverette. She wished Marsden would leave.

"Yeah," was all Leverette said not looking at her.

"Wonder if they're gonna find the rest of her today," she said. "So far we have her extremities."

"Don't know," Leverette said.

"We better get back and see what Gordon found out," Marsden said to pull them away from her.

She pouted. "Okay. See you later," she said , and threw her blonde ponytail behind her, looking at Leverette. She walked away with a deliberate sway in her hips. Leverette didn't even look her way.

The car was a few feet away and Leverette quickly walked toward it with Marsden in tow.

Once they got in Leverette said, "I wish she'd find a nice young man and leave me alone."

"She must like older men," Marsden said, and grinned. "Unless you find someone, she's going to think you're fair game."

"Not in her wildest dreams," Leverette said and started the car.

When they got back to the precinct, they noticed Gordon in with Billingsley. They were both sitting at Billingsley's desk and talking. When Billingsley saw Leverette and Marsden walk in, he motioned for them to come into his office.

"What's up?" Leverette asked as he sat in a chair next to Gordon. Marsden decided to stand.

Gordon didn't like Leverette and knew he knew. It wasn't that Leverette ever did anything, it was just his persona or aura He was just not comfortable when he was around.

"I couldn't find anything in common with the two names you gave me. No groups, church, employers, or friends in common. Once we find out who this woman was, we might be able to figure out something," Gordon said to the group.

"Well, we have two other names now. A DeShawn Davis and Shin Yoo. From what we know, Davis is a factory worker and Yoo works on computers," Marsden said.

Billingsley looked up at Marsden and noticed a hint of reservation in his eyes.

"What is it, Marsden?" the chief asked.

Marsden thought for a moment not wanting to sound like an idiot.

"I just get the feeling they're not telling us every-thing," Marsden said directly to Billingsley.

Billingsley nodded his head. He knew Marsden's gut feelings always had merit and he wondered if he wasn't psychic or something.

"Can you put a finger on it?" Billingsley asked.

"No. I was hoping maybe Gordon had something," Marsden finally sat in the chair next to Leverette. "I don't think they had anything to do with it, just that they know something."

"Best thing is to bring them in and talk to them," Billingsley said and sat back in his chair folding his arms in front of him. He thought for a minute. "We have four different people to talk to. We assume Lang and Dalton don't know each other. We'll have to see about Davis and Yoo. Do you get the same feeling with all of them, Marsden?"

"Yeah. When we spoke to Lang at first, I thought it

was just her being so shook up, but then there was just something she wasn't saying. I got the same feeling with the others, also."

"They had surveillance cameras around the factory, and we got a copy of the last twenty-four hours," Leverette said. "We'll go to see Andy and see what's on it."

The chief thought for a minute.

"Let Gordon check to see if there is a connection with the other two before we do anything. In the meantime, see if Carrington can tell us anything."

The three stood and Leverette said, "Okay."

As they walked out the chief's office, Gordon told Leverette and Marsden that he'd get right on it and let them know what he found.

As the two detectives walked to their desks Leverette said, "I'll give Carrington a call and see if it's worth our while to head out."

"Sure," was all Marsden said, dreading the trip to the morgue.

Leverette dialed and Marcie answered. He closed his eyes and Marsden knew it was her.

"I need to speak with Carrington," was all he said hoping Marcie wasn't going to try to get all cutesie on him like she usually did.

"He's examining the extremities right now. I can have him call you or you can just stop on over," she said with a hint of 'come-and-see-me' in her tone.

"No, just have him give me a call when he has something," Leverette said and hung up before she could say anything.

He looked over at Marsden.

"If you say a word, I'll send you to see Carrington yourself," he said.

Marsden just made a zipped motion across his lips but had a slight grin.

Chapter Ten

LEVERETTE AND MARSDEN walked into Andy's lab and, as usual, were amazed by all the electronic equipment he had. Shelves were lined with various types of electronic gadgets they didn't recognize.

Andy Clark had been with the force for thirteen years and was the best at what he did. He didn't look like someone who would know about computers or any other kind of electronics. He looked more like someone who should be on a farm. A good ol' boy, tall and muscular, who should be bailing hay instead of being tucked away in this lab.

"Hey, guys," Andy said in his bright chipper way. "Got something for me?"

"Yeah. Footage from some warehouse surveillance cameras," Marsden said. "How soon can you get to them?"

"Let me take a look now," he said and took the two

tapes Leverette handed him. "They still use tapes? They should upgrade. Glad I still have a tape player."

Leverette and Marsden knew he was just thinking out loud, something he was known for.

Andy rolled his chair to the other side of the desk he was sitting at and slipped the first of the two tapes into the machine and started it.

"At least its good quality," he said as it ran through the tape player. "Is there a specific time you're looking for?"

"We don't know for sure," Marsden said. "We think maybe earlier this morning."

"Oh, this is the dismembered body case," he said enthusiastically. "I was hoping something would come into my lab."

"So, you heard about it?" Leverette asked.

"You bet," Andy said. "And there's the body part. What was it? It looks small."

"An arm," was all Leverette said.

"Let me put the other tape in," he said, ejecting the first one and putting in the second. He fast forwarded to just before the time stamp on the first tape. As he got closer to the time, with Leverette and Marsden looking over his shoulders, he stopped the tape.

"There's a figure there," Marsden said. "Can you wind it back a bit?"

"You bet," Andy said and wound it back about ten minutes and let it play.

The three watched as a dark figure approached and looked up into the camera. It held up the arm as if taunting them. Then it walked the few steps to the pallets and laid it right on the top palette. It turned, looked back up at the camera, saluted and walked away.

"That fucking bastard," Leverette said. "His face was completely covered, and he had sunglasses on."

"Did they give you any other tapes?" Andy said. "Maybe I could see what vehicle he used."

Leverette had two other tapes marked 'parking lot' and handed them to Andy. He took the tapes and looked for the one that would correspond with the time stamp on the one they just watched. Andy took out that tape and put in the other. Again, they watched. Nothing. He didn't get into a vehicle just walked out of the parking lot.

"I can check with other area cameras and see if I can find anything," Andy said. "I'll give you a buzz if I do, or not."

"Thanks," Marsden said, and the two detectives left the lab.

McCullough called his boss and told him about what they found.

"Man, I can't do this today," he told his boss. "I'm shaking so hard I can hardly stand."

"How many cars are left?"

"Fifteen. We checked them all and this one was the only one with – someone in it," McCullough said. He felt like he was going to be sick.

"All right. I'll send Benton to finish up. I want them all moved today."

"Thanks, Boss," McCullough said and hung up. He

told his partner what he just spoke to their boss about then got in his truck and headed home.

He'd just made it through his door when it hit him, and he vomited into his toilet. He went to the sink to rinse out his mouth and put some cold water on his face. When he looked in the mirror, he saw how ashen he was and thought he'd lie down for a while.

After taking his boots off, he stretched out on his sofa trying to get the image out of his head. Then another image crept in: the dream he'd had last night. He watched a man put the body in the two plastic bags and then look him in the eye. The man put his fingers to his lips and made the "Shh" sound. In the dream McCullough heard an owl hoot three times and he woke up shaking. He looked at his clock and it was midnight.

What a fucked up dream, he thought as he opened his eyes. He wondered if he would ever forget it. All he wanted right now was to rest and not remember any of it.

Should he have told the detectives about the dream? No, they'd think he was crazy. He didn't want to tell anyone. He didn't want to admit it to himself!

Chapter Eleven

MARSDEN SAT at his desk going over the paperwork he had on the case. It was 2PM and they hadn't received any new information . He looked over at Leverette, who was on the phone with Carrington.

"No, we haven't heard anything yet," he said into the phone, rubbing his forehead. "Yeah. Gordon's doing a check on the four we already spoke to."

"I doubt all of them did it. The cuts are exactly the same," Carrington replied.

"Well, maybe one of them did it and the others lured her to an area," Leverette said sitting back in his chair. He looked across the desks and noticed Marsden listening to the conversation.

Leverette hung up the phone and looked at Marsden.

"Did you hear from Gordon yet?" he asked, folding his hands on his desk.

"Yeah. Amy Lang and Shin Yoo know each other'

they go to the same church. The other two don't know the others. They don't connect anywhere."

When Leverette looked past Marsden, he froze. Billingsley was walking toward them with misery written all over his face. He was hoping it wasn't another body part.

"Got the torso," Billingsley said and handed the file to Marsden. He took it reluctantly then handed it over to Leverette.

Leverette opened it and read the one-page report, then shook his head.

"Keeps going like this, we'll have the whole body today," Leverette said and handed the file back to Marsden.

"Well, you two get going. Carrington will be there soon, if he's not already," Billingsley said and walked back to his office.

"I'll sure be glad when this case is solved," Marsden whispered after Billingsley walked away. "This is creeping me out."

"Yes, I know. You don't exactly hide the fact," Leverette said with a grin on his face. "Let's get going."

The torso had been found in a car at an old junk yard. They turned into the drive and up to where they saw the squad car.

"Do I have to get out?" Marsden asked.

"Yes, we need to talk to the officers and the person who found it," Leverette said with a grin, and shook his head.

They headed to where the officers were standing. Carrington was leaning into the car on the driver's side and had removed the top bag.

"What do we have here?" Leverette asked.

"Might be related to the parts we found earlier today," Carrington said as he backed away from the car door. "Looks like the same type of saw marks."

"Who found it?" Leverette asked the officers. He recognized them as Murphy and Laurence.

"This guy, Frank McCullough. He and his buddy were supposed to move all these cars to the new location. He noticed something in the front seat and when he walked over, it smelled foul. When he touched the bag, it scared the hell out of him," Laurence said.

Leverette turned to the man. "Did you have gloves on?"

"Yes, he did. We always wear them when we're moving things," the man said. "We always check them for people because we've found some sleeping in them even in this cold."

"You're not McCullough?" Leverette asked.

"No, I'm Neil James. Frank left shortly after finding it. He looked like he was about to die. Mark Peterson came to give me a hand with the others."

"Well, you're not going to be moving any more cars today," Leverette said. "This place is now a crime scene. Once we're done you can finish."

"I'll call the boss and let him know," James said and pulled out his cell.

"Okay. We'll have to have McCullough come to the precinct to give a statement," Leverette said. The three men left, and Leverette headed to Carrington.

"She's probably our girl then," Leverette said.

"I'd bet my life on it," Carrington told him. "I saw some surgical scars, but I don't know if that'll tell us anything until I get her back to the morgue."

"Let me know what you find. We're going to be getting the five people in to talk to them tomorrow," Leverette said.

"Too bad we didn't find the headfirst," Carrington said. "Can you ask one of the officers to help me get her out?"

"Yeah," was all Leverette said and headed back to the car.

"Carrington needs one of you to help him get her out and into his van," Leverette said looking at the two officers.

"No problem. I'll go," Murphy said, and headed over to help Carrington.

Marsden wrote down everything James told him, including McCullough's phone number.

So far Gordon found out two of them knew each other, and the other two didn't know any of them. Was McCullough the connection?

Marsden happened to look where Carrington and Murphy were. He saw them almost drop the torso and he started feeling sick. He quickly looked back at his note pad and wrote a few other things down to get his mind off what he saw.

Leverette walked up and noticed Marsden's face pale and a little tremble in his hands.

"We can go, now," Leverette said. He didn't want to say more in front of James.

Marsden put his note pad and pen in his pocket and headed to the car.

"You okay?" Leverette asked.

"I will be when we get out of here," Marsden said and kept his eyes down. "Please, let's go."

Leverette started the car, then turned around and headed out.

"Carrington said he's sure it's the same woman," Leverette said. "The saw marks are identical. He said he saw a few surgical scars but won't know anything until he checks her out."

"I kinda figured it was," Marsden said trying not to remember what he just saw. "I'll be glad when we catch this bastard!"

"Me, too," Leverette said and headed back to the precinct.

When they arrived, Leverette went to talk to the chief and Marsden called Gordon with the new name.

"Hey Gordon," Marsden said. "We got another name for you to run."

"Okay, give it to me," Gordon said and picked up a pen.

"Frank McCullough. He works for Littleman's Salvage in Port Huron."

"Okay, I'll work my magic," Gordon said and hung up.

Marsden turned and saw Leverette talking to Billingsley and took a deep breath. He didn't want to talk about what they just found but he took the information. He should be in there. Reluctantly he got up and walked over.

"What'd he tell you, Marsden?" Billingsley asked.

"Just that they were relocating the cars to their new yard. They always check the cars for people who sleep in them and found the black bag."

"What did Carrington say?"

"He's positive it's our lady," Leverette said. "The saw marks are identical. He'll call when he's done."

"I gave Gordon the name of the guy who found it," Marsden said and swallowed hard. The image kept creeping into his mind.

Chapter Twelve

OSCAR SAT on his perch watching Carole make a sandwich for lunch. Once she finished and poured herself some tea, he jumped down and went to his food dish.

"You gonna have lunch with me?" Carole asked and smiled as he looked up at her and let out a gentle 'mew'.

She sat at the table and looked out at the melting snow scape, wishing spring would hurry and get here. It had been such a cold, snowy winter.

Just as she took a bite of her sandwich her cell phone rang. She looked at the caller ID and saw it was her friend Amy.

"Hey," she said with her mouth full.

"Sorry to bother you. Are you eating?" Amy said sounding upset.

"Yeah, no problem," Carole said and took a sip of tea to wash the food down. "What's wrong?"

"I was wondering if I could stop by after work and just talk," Amy's voice was full of fear.

"Sure. I'm off all week," Carole said. "I don't have any plans. Want to meet for dinner?"

"No. I need to talk to you. Alone."

"Okay. We can order pizza or Chinese if you want," Carole wasn't sure what was wrong, but obviously Amy really needed to speak to her.

"Either will be fine. I'll see you around 5:30."

"Sure. See you then," Carole said and hung up the phone. She had known Amy for about fifteen years and had never heard her sound like this. Something had really gotten to her. Carole couldn't put her finger on it.

Just then the feeling came rushing back , almost bringing her to her knees. She gripped her stomach. "What the hell?" she thought, as she bent over her kitchen table.

Carole started getting a vision but couldn't believe what she was seeing. It was a woman on a table with her arms, legs and head cut from her body. She saw the woman's face but didn't recognize her. The room looked dirty and only a light hanging over the body illuminated it.

Carole saw a figure, a man she thought, picking up each arm and leg and putting them in separate black plastic bags. Then, he took the head and bagged it too. He used two bags for the body tying what looked like twine around the middle of the body to secure the bags.

Then he looked at Carole. Dark, foreboding eyes stared right into hers. She could see a smile under the surgical mask. He brought up a finger to his mouth and said "Shh."

This snapped her out of it. She sat up and noticed Oscar's hair on end and his tail puffed.

"It's okay, baby," she said as he hesitantly walked to her. She reached down and petted him. He slowly started to relax.

"Poor thing," she said to him. "This bothers you, too, doesn't it?"

He mewed and rubbed against Carole's legs. She wondered if he felt the other little visions she got. Carole was never home when they hit. She was either at work or out when they came to her.

Carole sat back in her chair and closed her eyes for a second. She opened them and looked at her lunch. She picked up her sandwich and took another bite, thinking about what she'd just seen. She unconsciously took a sip of her tea and set the cup down.

There had been nothing outstanding in the room in her vision. There was one door on the wall to the left of the table the woman was on. Then there was another smaller table. She thought she saw a chain saw sitting on it, beside a box of trash bags.

The man, she was sure it was a man now, wore a rain suit that covered his clothing completely, a surgical cap, mask, and surgical gloves. He was careful, she thought, to not leave any evidence on the body, the bags or his own clothing.

She couldn't get those eyes out her head. Never had

she seen such dark, frightening eyes. Almost, what, hypnotic? So dark you couldn't see the pupils.

Carole finished her sandwich and got up to put the plate in the sink. She wanted to rearrange the closet in her second bedroom and thought that would be a good way to pass the time until Amy came over. She just wondered what was bothering her friend.

Carole, after finishing with the closet, saw it was getting late and decided to order pizza on-line and arranged for it to be delivered around 5:15PM. She had beer and soda pop in the fridge, so that was all set. Now she just had to wait for Amy to get there.

She sat and went over in her mind what she'd seen in the last feeling. The woman wasn't someone she knew, and Carole couldn't help wondering if she was alive when he cut her into pieces and hoped she wasn't. She remembered him looking directly into her eyes and shushing her. That really gave her the creeps. Did he know her? She knew she didn't know him because she'd remember those eyes. She would remember someone like that. Was he even real? Maybe he just represented someone else. But that poor woman!

Carole jumped when doorbell rang. It was either the pizza or Amy.

She went to look through the peep hole and saw that it was Amy. It was just a little past five. The look of fear on her face made Carole open the door quickly.

"Come on in," Carole said, holding the door open. Amy walked in and closed the outer door.

"Damn, is this weather ever going to let up?" Amy said and shivered as Carole shut the inner door behind her.

"Might not get spring until June if this keeps up," Carole said trying to lighten Amy's mood. "I can put some coffee on. The pizza should be here soon."

"Yeah, that sounds like a plan," Amy said, soberly as if she were a million miles away. She took her hat, scarf and coat off and hung them on the nearby coat rack. She wrapped her arms around herself and walked to the kitchen table and sat down.

Carole finished with the coffee maker and sat across from her friend. She saw Amy had a wild look in her eyes.

"Now, tell me what's going on," Carole said.

Amy thought for a minute, still appearing as though she were somewhere else. She knew Carole had some sort of intuition or something. Maybe she could tell her what the dream meant. She took a deep breath.

"To be honest, I feel silly about all this," Amy started. "This morning I was walking Bud like I always do before work. He got upset and pulled me to the bank. I saw a black trash bag with red painted toenails sticking out of it."

Carole gasped. She remembered the woman had red painted nails.

Amy saw Carole's reaction. "Has it been on the news?" she asked Carole.

"No. Not that I heard. I had the local radio station on all day," Carole said. "That must have been horrible for you. No wonder you're so upset."

Amy, who had her hands folded on the table, began to tremble. Carole reached across the table and put her hands over Amy's.

"It'll take time to get that out of your head," Carole said.

"It's not just that," Amy said not pulling back from Carole. "The one detective made me feel like he didn't believe me. "

"That's the way they work," Carole said. The coffee was ready, and she got up to make a cup for each of them. "They don't have any idea and you found it..." Carole trailed off. "You didn't see anything did you? Is someone threatening you to keep quiet?"

Carol brought the coffee to the table.

Amy looked directly into Carole's eyes.

"You saw something?" Carole's eyes widened.

"No. Not really," Amy said debating whether to say anything. "I had a dream last night."

"Tell me about it."

Amy hung her head. "You're going to think I'm crazy."

"No, I won't," Carole assured her. "Tell me, please. It's okay."

Amy took a deep breath. "I dreamt about that leg last night. I saw the woman on a table, all cut up and a man putting the leg in a black bag. Then he looked me in the eye and shushed me."

Anxiety built in Carole's chest and her head started to spin. "What?" Her voice was choked with fear.

She looked down at her coffee and jumped when the

doorbell rang. She cleared her throat, trying to push past her feelings. "Must be the pizza," she said and got up to get the door.

While she was gone Amy started wonder if Carole thought she was crazy. Could she think she had something to do with it?

Carole came back into the kitchen and put the pizza box on the table.

She looked over at Amy who slowly brought her head up to look Carole in the eyes.

"I didn't have anything to do with it," Amy said with tears in her eyes. "That detective made me feel like I was hiding something from him."

"I know you didn't. They have a job to do. I had a weird dream, too," Carole said not wanting to let on about her feelings.

"Really?"

"Yes. Only I saw a woman, like you did, and the man putting each of her parts into black plastic bags."

"That's terrible! Did he look up at you, too?" Amy started to relax a little bit, now that she knew someone else had seen it

"Yeah, once he finished with the whole body," Carole sighed. "Scared the shit out of me!"

"Me, too! I just don't know why it happened to me," Amy said and took a slice of pizza.

Carole reached into the box and took a slice, also. She reached for two napkins and handed one to Amy.

"Did you recognize the woman?" Amy asked between bites.

"No. And I didn't recognize that man. Those eyes were so dark, I'd know if I knew him, and I'd be able to identify him."

"I'm afraid if I tell the police, they'll think I knew something about it," Amy put her pizza slice down and took a sip of her coffee. "They want to talk to me again."

The room became silent and suddenly Amy's cell phone rang. They both jumped and then smiled at their reactions.

"Hello," Amy answered.

"Hello, Ms. Lang? This is Detective Marsden. I'm sorry to call you so late but I was wondering if you could come in tomorrow morning?" He didn't mention they found all the limbs and the torso.

Carole saw the color slip from Amy's face and her hands begin to shake.

"Sure, what time?" she asked hoping her voice didn't give away her nervousness.

"Around 9AM?"

"Yes, I'll be there."

"Good. See you then," Marsden said and hung up.

Amy shut off her phone and locked it before putting it back in her purse. She was pale and still shaking.

"They want me to come in and talk to them tomorrow morning." She looked up at Carole, the fear evident in her eyes.

"I wouldn't worry," Carole said trying to calm her

friend. "They probably just want to go through everything again. After a good night's rest, you might remember something."

"A good night's rest?" Amy said shocked. "I don't think I'll ever sleep again. What if I see him again?"

"You probably won't unless your own subconscious brings it up," Carole tried to reassure her.

"Probably? I know I will. How do you know he won't come back in my dreams?"

Carole realized she had better tell Amy about her feelings. She looked down at her plate contemplating where to start. Then she looked up.

"When I was thirteen, I had a feeling and a type of vision that I later learned was the same ones my mother had. My great-aunt had died, and the feeling and vision was about her," Carole looked directly in Amy's eyes to be sure she was following. "Ever since, I've had these feelings and pictures."

"You mean you know when people are going to die?" Amy was intrigued.

"Yes, or just after they die. Today the feeling made me double over like I was sucker-punched in the gut. Then I saw the woman and that man. He was putting her body parts into black trash bags. Then he looked me right in the eye and shushed me."

"Oh my God! You saw him too! Why don't you come with me tomorrow?"

"I don't think the police are interested in my feelings and visions. They think of us as quacks."

"But you could back up my dream," Amy pleaded.

"They'll probably think you coached me. No, I can't go," Carole picked up her coffee cup and took a sip. It was getting cold.

"You *won't* go you mean," Amy was getting angry. "What if they don't think you're a quack? You saw the whole body and him."

"They have no idea who this woman was?"

"No. They only found the arm as far as I know. They didn't say anything else about it."

Carole thought for a moment. "They might think I'm the one who did it, or that I know the man who did," she was fighting a battle in her mind. She wanted to help her friend but also wanted to stay out of jail. Her better side won. "All right, I'll go. Let's just hope the detectives have open minds."

Amy's face brightened, but only a little. She still felt sick inside. "I have to be there by 9:00, so I'll come pick you up."

"Okay. Let's finish this pizza. Do you want some more coffee?"

"Sure," Amy said feeling a lot better about facing the next day.

Chapter Thirteen

A BLACK SHADOW was hiding the curve-ahead markers in Bearss Hills. He knew how the kids come barreling down the road and this would work just fine.

He picked up the black bag he was carrying and checked for traffic. Nothing. He ran across the two-lane road and agilely climbed a tree. The curve would bring any speeder right to this spot so he placed the bag into the split of the tree and secured it a bit. He didn't want it to fall too soon.

After he got down and crossed back over the road, a car came roaring along. That was close. He had just enough time to hide behind the trees. Then he heard the wheels screeching to stop, but it was not soon enough. The car crashed into the tree and, just as he hoped, the head fell out of the tree and landed on the roof of the car.

Slowly he crept through the woods to where he'd hidden his car, got in and called 911.

"911. What is your emergency?" a male voice asked.

"Some kids just crashed into a tree in Bearss Hills," he said, forcing mock emotion into his voice.

"Are they all right?"

"I don't know. I'm handicapped and have trouble getting in and out of my car. You better send someone." He hung up before the man could ask any questions.

Leverette, home in bed sleeping and dreaming about his late wife and son, jumped when his phone rang. He looked at the clock: 3 a.m. What now?

He picked up the phone and trying not to sound sleepy, said hello.

"This is Carter at the precinct. There was an accident in Bearss Hills, and they need you there," he said.

"For an accident? Why do you need homicide?" Leverette sat up on the side of his bed.

"We think we found your lady's head," Carter said.

"That's a good reason. Did you call Billingsley?"

"Yes, he said to get you and Marsden down here and then he'd meet up with you at the precinct," Carter said sounding a little shaken up.

"Okay. I'll give Marsden a call and we'll be there as soon as we can. Bye," He hung up and dialed Marsden. It rang a couple times before he picked up.

"Yeah," Marsden said through a yawn.

"They think they found her head, we gotta go to Bearss Hills," Leverette said as he slipped into his jeans balancing his cell with his shoulder.

"Where the hell is that?" Marsden asked, still lying in bed, wondering if he was dreaming.

"I know where it's at. I'll pick you up. Your place is on the way," Leverette hung up and finished dressing.

"Hello? Hello? Damn that man," Marsden said and got out of bed. He was so hoping they would have found the head before the shift was over. Now they'd get to see it, in the dark, in a place he didn't know. Shit!

He started to dress and felt a very cold chill go through his body. Why couldn't they find the head during the day? Shit!

Leverette showed up about fifteen minutes later and Marsden was waiting, looking out his front window. It was still cold out, even though it was supposed to be getting warm. Damn winter took it's time leaving.

Marsden put on his hat and coat, then his gloves. He knew it was a lot colder at night and thought about putting a scarf around his mouth like his mother used to make him do when he was little.

He got in the car and was grateful it was warm.

"What do you know about it?" he asked Leverette.

"Not much. A car missed the curve and plowed into a tree. The head fell on the car's roof," Leverette answered.

Marsden shivered. They sat in silence and Marsden looked out the window trying to figure out where they were. "Boy, this road changes names a lot," he said. "How do you know where to go?"

"Fortunately, the crash is right by the canoe dock,"

Leverette said. "We used to go there a lot. My son loved canoeing."

Marsden felt bad. He knew Leverette had lost his wife and son in a car accident a while back. He didn't say anything more.

The flashing lights on the cruiser were easy to find in the sparsely lit area. Leverette parked next to the cruiser and the two men got out. Marsden only walked to the front of the car and stopped.

Leverette turned and noticed his partner wouldn't move.

"What?" Leverette asked.

"I'll wait here," is all Marsden said as he wrapped his scarf around his neck and mouth.

Leverette shook his head and went to the site of the crash.

"Okay, what do we have?" he asked the officers.

"Looks like they missed the curve. Fortunately, they weren't going too over the limit. All three got out of the car as we pulled up," one officer said. Leverette didn't know him. "Angie, I mean Officer Buckley, saw the bag on top of the car and when she went to grab it, she jumped back."

"Yes, Detective. I did. When I grabbed the bag, I felt what I thought was a nose," she said to him. Before he could ask, she added, "I had my gloves on, sir."

Leverette nodded. "And the passengers? Did they see or hear anything?"

"All they said was after the crash they heard something hit the roof. They got out about the time we got here and didn't touch anything."

"They said they weren't hurt, just a little shook up."

Leverette turned to look at the other side of the road and noticed all but one of the three curve markers were covered with brush. He turned to the officers.

"Did you see these?" he said pointing to the markers.

"Yes, sir. We took a picture of them. When we went over to see them it looked like the tree branches were tied down to them. One must have not been tied good enough, so it came off," the male officer said.

Leverette couldn't see his name because of his overcoat.

"Get the rope to the lab," Leverette said almost to himself. He turned and headed back across the street to where the boys were standing. Once the officers got the ropes down and bagged them, they followed Leverette across the street.

"I know you just told these officers what happened, but tell me now," he said as gently as he could.

The boys were not only worried about the accident but when the officers whispered to each other about the black bag on the roof they got scared.

Leverette noticed their apprehension and felt bad for them.

"Okay. Which one of you was driving?"

"I was, sir; my name is Phillip King. These are my friends John Stephens and Michael Clark." King said and swallowed hard.

"Did you notice anyone in the area before or after the crash?"

All three of them shook their heads. They were starting to feel the cold and shivered .

"Is it all right if I go get our jackets, sir?" King asked.

"I'll let the officer get them for you," Leverette said and waved one of the officers over and told her to get their coats. He waited until they all put their coats on and continued with the questions.

"You didn't see the curve markers?"

"No, sir, I wasn't even going that fast, but I guess the road was more slippery than I thought because I couldn't correct the car in time," King said.

"Well, it's obvious this wasn't your fault. Someone deliberately set this up and you just happened to be the one caught.

"Can you tell my father that, sir?" King asked hopefully.

"Sure thing. We'll let him know everything," Leverette said and imagined his own son at this age.

The coroner's van pulled up and Leverette turned to see who it was. *Shit*, he thought to himself. Marcie! He should have figured Carrington wouldn't get his fat ass out of bed.

"Hi Detective," she sang. .

"The officer will show you where the head is," Leverette said without thinking.

"Head? That's a head on top of my car?" King started shaking uncontrollably.

"Let's go over here," Leverette said wanting to kick himself in the ass for not thinking. He led the boys to where Marsden was standing. "He'll write down what you tell him. Your father's been called, so he should be here soon," Leverette said and, hesitantly, walked back to the officers, and Marcie.

Steeling himself for Marcie's advances, he asked Buckley if they'd seen anything else by the markers.

"No. No footprints, no cigarette butts, nothing," she said.

Marcie had taken the head down and walked over to where one of the overhead lights were. She put the bag down and opened it.

"Yup," Marcie said. "It's a head. We won't know anything until we get her back to the lab."

"What time is Carrington coming in?" Leverette asked.

"I don't know, usually around 9 am. I was going back there and, if you like, you could wait for him with me."

Not on your life. "No, that's okay. I have to get Marsden back to his place," was all he said.

"You sure?" she said, trying to sound sexy.

"I'm sure," he answered and headed to where Marsden and the others were standing. He thought she must be nuts. Wanting to make out, or whatever the kids call it now, in the morgue? Fuck no! Not with her or anyone else. The thought sent a shudder through his whole body.

A mid-size SUV pulled up to the patrol car. The man

who came out was huge, not fat, but well over six foot, and quite muscular.

"That's my dad," King said still shaking.

"What happened?" He growled at his son.

"Mr. King, I'm Detective Leverette. This wasn't your son's fault. It was set up."

"How's that? Set up? By who?" Mr. King turned his anger toward Leverette.

"We don't know who, sir, all we know is that the curve markers were covered, and..."

"And a head fell out of the tree on my car," his son interrupted.

"What?" Mr. King went from angry to almost terrified. "A head?"

"Yes, Mr. King. We can't say more about the case," Leverette said.

"The car?"

"Your son wasn't going over the speed limit. There's little damage on the front," Marsden said.

"What about that head? Whose head is it?" Mr. King was visibly shaken.

"We can't discuss..."

"Yeah, yeah, it's an open case. I know. Is the car drivable?"

"I think it is, but we need to take it to get any evidence from the tree that might have fallen with the head. Then it'll be brought to your home," Leverette told him. "It shouldn't take more than a day, two at most."

Mr. King put his hands on his hips and let out a sign. "Fine."

"Here's my card if you have any questions," Leverette said and handed over his card. "You can call me to find out when your car is ready if you don't hear from us."

"Okay boys, let's go," Mr. King said to the three young men. They got into the car and headed home. John and Mike live next door to each other, so they were dropped off first.

Paul King turned to his son and noticed how badly he's been shaken up.

"That must have been horrible," he said as compassionately as he could.

"I was all right until I heard about the head. We just thought a branch fell from the tree, Dad," Phil said.

"They told you about the head?" Paul started getting upset.

"No, no. We overheard them talking about it. They didn't know we moved up to where they were standing. The one detective was pretty pissed that we heard."

Phil couldn't stop shaking. His father could understand his being this bothered, but he should have calmed down a little by now.

"Is there something else? I'm not mad about the car, you guys weren't hurt, and the car's not bad."

Phil tried to relax. How could he tell his father? How would he react?

"Dad, do you believe dreams can predict things?"

"Your mother's the one who believes all that, shit. Why?"

Phil sighed. "Last night I had a dream that this guy put a woman's head in a black plastic bag. His face was covered so all I could see were his eyes. He looked me in the eye and shushed me. Then I heard an owl hoot three times. I was so scared I woke up; it was midnight."

Paul King stared out the windshield. He felt a chill.

"Dad?"

"I believe you," his father said. "Just don't tell your mother, about either of them." He glanced at his son and the two of them chuckled.

Chapter Fourteen

LEVERETTE AND MARSDEN got into the car and pulled away as Marcie was putting the head in the van. She turned to blow Leverette a kiss but he was already gone. *Damn*, she thought, *I'll win him over sooner or later.*

The ride to Marsden's home started out quiet until Leverette decided to find out why this case was bothering Marsden so much.

"You have no trouble with all the other gory cases we go on, why does this one get to you?" he asked trying not to sound condescending.

Marsden stared out his side window for a bit then turned to Leverette.

"It happened when I was nine. My father was working on a combine and it jammed. Instead of turning it off he jumped down and reached into it to loosen whatever it was," Marsden turned away. He didn't want his partner to see the tears in his eyes. "Our neighbor, whose land butts up to ours in the back, noticed the combine running and saw Dad on the ground. He ran over and saw what happened. Dad's right arm and leg were severed off. He got caught in the machine. The neighbor ran to our house and told my mother to call for an ambulance and let her know what happened. She called then started out the door, but he stopped her, telling her she didn't want to see him. But Mom was stubborn, still is, and headed out the door with me following. We didn't know Dad was dead. He was just lying there."

Leverette didn't know what to say. He couldn't imagine a boy that young seeing that. He knew what loss felt like.

"I'm so sorry, Phil," Leverette said.

His sincerity, and the fact he called him by his first name, touched him. "Thanks, Joe."

"Is that why you didn't carry on with the family farm?"

"No. I always wanted to be a cop," Marsden said looking back over at Leverette. "My brothers and sister took over the farm. They were already out of high school, so they took over right away."

Leverette nodded as they pulled up to Marsden's home.

"Get some sleep. I'll see you in a couple hours," Leverette said.

Marsden looked at him. "Really? I don't think I'll ever sleep again," he said. "Are you going home?"

"Probably," Leverette answered him.

"You're going to the precinct," Marsden said. "I know you better than that." He got out of the car. Before he shut the door, he said, "I'll be right behind you."

"Okay, see you there," Leverette said.

Marsden shut the door and walked into his home.

After Leverette parked his car and walked into the precinct he looked to see if there was any coffee. *Shit. No.* He put on a pot and went to his desk.

He turned on his computer and took his coat off, hanging it on his chair. He sat down and opened his drawer taking out the five files for the case. Today they were going to start interviewing the witnesses. Hopefully, they'd have a name before the interviews start.

Leverette checked his email. Carrington had sent him his notes on his findings. He wondered if Carrington was going to come in or let Marcie handle it. It's not that she didn't know what to do, after all she was the assistant ME, Leverette just couldn't stand her.

He opened the file and it confirmed what he thought: same cut pattern. He remembered Marcie said the cut pattern on the neck looked like the cuts on the rest of the body.

The rest of the report stated that she hadn't been sexually assaulted, nor did she have any bruises except the strap marks that had bound her ankles and wrists, and tighter marks just below her shoulders and at the top of her hips. Carrington did find ether in her system, so

Leverette knew she was knocked out and probably not gagged.

A chill went through Leverette as he thought about the murder. Carrington said it looked like she had been alive when she was cut. He wondered if she was awake when he started cutting her. He wondered if she saw the blade coming down on her neck. But could she have survived if he cut her limbs off first? He'd have to wait for the report.

Marsden walked in and headed for the coffee pot.

"Want some?" he asked Leverette.

"Yeah. I just put it on," he answered.

Marsden poured two cups and brought them over, handing one to Leverette. They both liked their coffee black.

"Anything new on the case?" Marsden asked as he set his coffee on his desk and took off his hat and coat. He threw them on the chair on the side of his desk.

"Nope," Leverette said still staring at the screen. "Gordon didn't find anything, either. Maybe now that we might get her ID'd, he'll find something."

"Is Marcie doing the exam on the head?" Marsden asked.

Leverette looked at him and gave him a mean look.

"Hey, I'm not trying to start anything. Just a simple question."

"Carrington said he wanted to do the whole examination," Leverette said and sat back in his chair. He picked up his coffee and took a sip.

"I have some of the witnesses scheduled for today.

Amy Lang, Ken Denton, and DeShawn Davis," Marsden said looking at his notes.

"I've been meaning to ask you," Leverette started, "Did you get your gut feeling with any of the boys today?"

"Yes," Marsden said. "The King kid knows something."

"Why?"

"Because when he heard 'head' I saw both fear and recognition on his face."

"But he's just a kid. What could he do?" Leverette could believe the other five might have done something, but not a seventeen-year-old.

"With all the shit going on in this world now, I wouldn't put it past him."

"They all looked frightened."

"Could be an act," Marsden said and turned on his computer. His emails were cc'd from Carrington and Gordon.

Leverette's cell phone rang, making Marsden jump. Leverette looked at him with a scowl on his face and shook his head. When he looked at the phone it was the morgue. The scowl went to an 'oh shit' look. He handed the phone to Marsden.

"It's the morgue," he said.

Marsden looked at him.

"Why don't *you* take it?" Marsden asked, then remembered Marcie was in the morgue so he took the phone.

"Marsden."

"Oh, I'm sorry," Marcie's voice came over the phone. "I was calling Joe."

Marsden looked at Leverette and grinned.

"He's not at his desk right now. How can I help you?"

"Dr. Carrington will be here in about an hour. I just wanted him to know."

"I'll tell him when he gets back."

"Oh, okay," she said, sounding disappointed. "Bye."

"Bye." Marsden hung up and handed the phone back to Leverette.

"She said Carrington will be in around 6 a.m," Marsden said. "She sounded upset that you didn't answer the phone."

Leverette just glared at him. "I really don't care."

"Sorry," Marsden said with a smirk on his face. "I didn't mean to upset you. We have enough to worry about."

"Thank you," Leverette said and finished going through his emails. As he opened the last email, he noticed the lights come on in Billingsley's office. He looked up and saw him take off his hat and coat and hook them on the coat rack. Then he walked toward Leverette and Marsden.

"How old's the coffee?" Billingsley asked.

"Just made it a few minutes ago," Leverette said.

"Good," Billingsley said and headed over to pour himself a cup. He walked back over to the two detectives. "Anything new?"

"Carrington will be in shortly. Gordon hadn't found anything connecting the five witnesses."

"Well, maybe once we learn who this woman was, we'll get somewhere," Billingsley said and turned and headed to his office.

Chapter Fifteen

LEVERETTE AND MARSDEN spent the early morning hours trying to figure out the case. Not knowing who the dead woman was made the investigation come to a halt.

"I wonder how bad the head was," Marsden said, shuddering at the thought.

"I didn't see it," Leverette said. "Marcie didn't say much at the scene. We'll have to wait for pictures and for Gordon to run it through his facial program, if it's not too bad, that is."

Marsden folded his arms in front of him and squeezed his eyes shut trying to get the picture out of his mind.

"Gordon's already working on the Kings," Leverette said. He noticed Gordon coming in, not looking sleep weary, and head right to his lab.

Leverette's cell rang again. He closed his eyes and shook his head hoping it wasn't Marcie again. When he looked at the caller ID, it was Gordon.

"Well, speak of the devil," Leverette said.

"Oh? Talking about me now," Gordon laughed. "Nothing on the Kings. Do you know when I'm going to get a picture of the head to run it through the facial recognition program?"

"Carrington should be there now. I'll have Marsden call and see what's up."

"Sounds like a plan," Gordon said and hung up.

"Okay, I'll call," Marsden said with a small grin on his face. He picked up his phone and called.

"Carrington," the ME answered.

"Hi, Doc, are we able to get a picture of the woman?"

"Yeah, you can come down and take one," Carrington said. "We can talk about some things I think I understand now."

Marsden swallowed hard. "Okay. Great.". He turned to Leverette and said, "We can go take the pictures now, and he wants to talk to us."

Leverette closed his eyes and bowed his head. *Shit.* Marsden couldn't handle the corpse and he couldn't handle Marcie.

"Come on," Leverette said. "I'll take the pictures and talk to the doc and you keep Marcie away from me. I've got the camera." He opened the lower drawer on the right side of his desk and pulled out the camera.

"Sounds good to me," Marsden said.

They both put their coats on and headed out the door.

The ride wasn't too bad since they didn't get any more snow, but it was still very cold. It took them thirty minutes to get there but it felt like only five to Leverette. He parked the car and the two detectives headed to the morgue. The warmth greeted them, and Marsden let out a sigh.

"This is better," he said.

Leverette just looked at him.

"I mean the heat."

"I know what you meant," Leverette said and walked up to the window. "We're here to see Dr. Carrington."

"Okay, Detective. I'll give him a call to let him know you're here," she said and dialed the number. As she told whoever answered the phone about their arrival, Leverette started thinking about the case. It really had him and everyone else baffled, especially the one tape they saw where the killer taunted them. "Fucking bastard!"

"You can go on ahead, detectives," the young lady said. She had her eyes on Marsden noticing how handsome he was.

They got to the morgue and Marsden said to Leverette, "Age before beauty," and chuckled.

"Right," was all Leverette said. Just as he was about to push one of the doors open Barb came out.

"Oh, I'm sorry," she said. "I hope I didn't hit you."

"No, I saw you coming," Leverette said and smiled at her. *Why can't Marcie be more like her?*

"He's waiting for you," Barb said and walked past them with folders in her arms.

Leverette took a deep breath and pushed the door open. He didn't see Marcie and felt relieved.

"Okay guys," Carrington said. "I think I know how she was killed."

Marsden hugged the wall by the doors. Leverette walked up to the table where the woman was lying. He noticed her face wasn't bruised at all so they should get a good picture for Gordon.

"Tell me," Leverette said.

"See these marks here?" Carrington said pointing to the marks on the torso. "I believe he had her limbs tied with a tourniquet of some sort. Then he'd cut off each limb, maybe waiting a few minutes between them."

The two men were startled when they heard a thump on the floor. They turned to see Marsden had passed out.

"Oh my," Marcie said from the side room in the morgue. "Poor thing." She grabbed a clean towel and ran it under water and went to put it on his forehead.

"You got that?" Carrington asked.

"Yeah, for now," Marcie answered. "I might not be able to get him up by myself." Her voice was starting to sound taunting.

"Well, let him be, then," Carrington said. "I'll finish here and let Leverette take the pictures he needs."

Marcie pouted but kept the towel on Marsden's head.

"Thanks, Doc," Leverette whispered.

"Oh, I know how she pines for you," Carrington said. He looked at Leverette with a grin on his face. "Anyway, I believe he cut off her head while she was alive. Probably enjoyed the fear in her eyes. Then he released the tourniquets and let her bleed out."

"Damn," Leverette said.

"She's a natural blonde, as you can tell," Carrington said, making Leverette blush. "But she dyed her hair black. Her eyes are blue. I'm going to do a dental plaster and search the dental database."

"Good. That'll help," Leverette said. He walked over to her head. "Can you lower the table so I can take pictures?"

"I can hold her head for you. The table doesn't work that well," Carrington said and picked her head up making Leverette cringe.

Carrington held it front first and Leverette took several pictures. He then turned it to the right for Leverette and then to the left. Gently he placed it back on what Leverette figured to be a morgue pillow.

"Good. These should help," Leverette said. They looked over at Marsden who was starting to wake.

"We're done here," Leverette said walking over to him and giving him a hand up.

"What happened?" Marsden asked, confused as he tried to maintain his balance.

"You fainted," Leverette said with a chuckle, doing everything he could to avoid Marcie's eyes.

"Really? I don't remember," Marsden said and looked at the table with the woman's body. "Let's go before I do it again."

Carrington called Marcie over so the two detectives could leave. She looked over at Leverette who kept his back to her.

Once they got back into the car, Leverette let out a sigh of relief.

"Why can't she find a nice young man?" he asked Marsden. "Someone closer to her own age. I'm old enough to be her father!"

"Your charm and wit must do something for her," Marsden teased. Leverette shot him an angry look. This made Marsden laugh out loud.

"That is not funny at all," Leverette said and started the car. This made Marsden laugh even harder.

Chapter Sixteen

AMY LANG and Carole Sage walked into the precinct and told the officer at the desk they were here to see Detective Marsden. The officer called Marsden to let him know two women were here to see him "Okay, thanks," Marsden said and hung up the phone with a puzzled look on his face.

"What?" Leverette asked.

"Two women are here to see me. I was only expecting one," he said and stood up.

"Maybe she needed a ride," Leverette said, "Or moral support."

"Yeah, maybe," Marsden shrugged his shoulders and headed to the front of the precinct. He saw Amy Lang and the other woman and walked up to them.

"Ms. Lang," he said politely, "Please come with me. Your friend can wait here." He pointed to a row of chairs along the wall. Carole went to sit down, and Amy went with Marsden.

He led Amy into an interrogation room on the left where Leverette was waiting with the file.

"You remember Detective Leverette?" he asked her.

"Yes. Hello," Amy said, getting more and more nervous.

Marsden pulled out a chair for her to sit. He then went across the table next to Leverette. Both detectives noticed how uncomfortable she was.

"Now, Ms. Lang, we just want to go over what you already told us. And to ask if you've remembered anything since yesterday morning," Marsden started in his soothing voice.

Amy wondered if the other detective was the bad cop. He looked like he could be.

"I just went to walk my dog and get a little exercise before going in to work," she said swallowing hard.

"You don't remember hearing or seeing anything out of the ordinary?" Leverette asked harshly.

Yup, he's the bad cop.

"Other than the leg, no. I didn't see or hear anything."

Leverette put his elbows on the table and intertwined his fingers resting his chin on them. He stared at her for a moment looking directly into her eyes.

"Are you sure you're telling us everything?" he asked.

Amy shuddered. "I, I, I," she couldn't finish her thought. How was she going to tell them she saw the woman in her dream, and the killer, too?

"You what?" Leverette said and slammed his fists on the tabletop. This made Amy jump and start to cry.

Marsden offered her some tissues to wipe her eyes. "Please forgive my partner. He tends to get a bit rough during interviews."

She wiped her eyes and tried to stop crying. For a few minutes she tried to get up the courage to tell them. So, what if they thought she was a nut job? Carole was there to help her out.

"I, I had a dream the night before," she started, not knowing if she could go on.

"What was the dream about, Ms. Lang?" Marsden asked his voice, still gentle.

She looked up at him and avoided Leverette. Marsden made her feel like she could tell him everything.

"I saw the murderer in my dream," she said at last. "But his face was covered except for his eyes."

Marsden and Leverette exchanged glances.

"I knew you'd think I was crazy!" Amy yelled. "I saw the woman on a steel table all cut up. I saw that man put her left leg in a black plastic bag and tie it off. Then he looked me in the eye and shushed me. Then an owl hooted three times!" She burst into tears.

The detectives didn't know what to think about this. They had worked with psychics on a couple cases, but this was different.

"Why didn't you tell us this before?" Marsden asked.

"The way you just looked at each other is why. You

think I'm nuts!" she yelled. "Carole Sage can tell you. She saw the whole thing!"

"And who is Carole Sage?" Leverette asked trying to tone his voice down.

"She came in with me. She's a sensitive or something. Carole saw the whole thing," Amy started sobbing again.

Leverette bristled. This Carole Sage might be someone to talk to.

"We'll be right back, Ms. Lang," Marsden said and handed her the box of tissues.

They were baffled by what they just heard.

"A sensitive saw the whole thing?" Marsden asked. "I wonder if she's part of it."

"I don't know. Maybe we should talk to her before we get to the other five," Leverette said. "She might have just dreamed it like Ms. Lang.

"You know I don't believe in that shit," Marsden said. "Even though we had that psychic help us with a couple cases."

"Yeah. She was good."

"I still don't believe," Marsden said and went back into the interrogation room.

Amy had calmed down, but her eyes were puffy from crying. She looked up at Marsden who smiled.

"Do you think we could talk to your friend?" he asked.

"Yeah. We talked about it last night," Amy said. "She didn't think it'd help but she said she would."

"Okay. Come with me. I'll show you to the lady's

room so you can freshen up. Then I'll go get her," Marsden said and held the door open for her.

He headed to the waiting area to get Carole.

"Ms. Sage, could you come with me, please?" Marsden asked.

Carole got up.

"Where's Amy?" she asked.

"She's in the lady's room. She'll meet you out here when we're done."

Marsden motioned for her to go down the hall and into the same room Amy had been in. Leverette was still there. He had called to have Gordon check Carole out and get the information to him as quickly as possible as soon as Marsden had led Ms. Lang out of the room.

It didn't take Gordon very long. "Looks like a good ol' girl. A couple parking tickets and one for speeding, but nothing criminal."

"Okay, Gordon, thanks," Leverette said and hung up the phone as Carole and Marsden entered the room.

Marsden held the chair out for Carole to sit in then rejoined his partner on the other side of the table. The three looked at each other for a bit.

"Ms. Lang said you have psychic powers or some such," Marsden said.

Carole took a slight breath and began.

"I'm not psychic; I get feelings and visions," she said steeling herself for the questions.

"Then what would you call yourself?" Marsden asked.

Leverette just sat there watching and listening.

"I don't know," she thought for a second, "I think I'm a sensitive."

Marsden looked at Leverette who was still looking at Carole. Carole became uncomfortable under the scrutiny.

Marsden looked back at Carole, who met his gaze.

"When did you see this – vision?"

"Yesterday, around noon," she said waiting for *the* question. "I was having my lunch."

Leverette sat quietly and this began to bother Marsden. Leverette was usually the one who played bad cop.

"Why don't you tell us about this vision?"

"I didn't see the actual murder," she started. "The woman was on the table already cut up. A man was putting each piece into its own bag."

"Can you describe the woman?" Leverette finally asked but gently.

Marsden didn't react to him but made a mental note to ask him about it.

"Did you see anyone else?" Leverette asked.

"Yes, there was a man there."

"Can you describe him?"

"Not really. He was in scrubs or something and had a cap and face mask on. All I could see were his eyes."

"What about the room? Do you remember anything you saw there?"

Carole felt odd. Were they making fun of her or seriously listening to what she was saying?

She thought for a minute.

"I saw the woman on a metal looking table and small tray table on the left."

"Her left?" Marsden asked.

"Yes. Her head was toward me. The walls were an ugly gray and there was a light over the table she was on."

Marsden was writing and then looked up at her. He noticed the concern in her eyes.

"Is something wrong, Ms. Sage?" he asked.

"You're taking this all in rather well," she said.

"We've worked with psychics before," Leverette said. "They were a big help."

"But I'm not a psychic…" she started to say.

"Yes, we know. But you may just very well be the one who helps us solve this case," Leverette said with a timid smile.

This made Carole blush and she smiled back.

"That's all I saw," she said and looked back at Marsden.

"Okay," Marsden said, "We'll be right back." He got up but Leverette was still sitting and looking at Carole. He tapped his shoulder.

"Oh, I'm coming," Leverette said feeling a little embarrassed.

The two men went out of the room and shut the door.

"What's with you?" Marsden asked.

"What do you mean?" Leverette asked.

"Did you hear anything she said?"

"Yeah," Leverette said, and that grin came back.

Marsden looked at him surprised and grinned back.

"You like her?"

"No," Leverette said and looked through the one-way window. "Why?"

"You look like…" Marsden stopped to think of a word. "You're smitten."

"Bull shit," Leverette said and looked at him not grinning anymore.

"You know the rules," Marsden said matter-of-factly.

"What the hell are you talking about?"

"You can't ask her out until after the case is solved."

"What makes you think I want to ask her out?"

Marsden just shook his head. He didn't like getting Leverette mad and he knew he was pissing him off.

"You're the one who believes in this nonsense," Marsden said changing the subject, "Do you think she's telling the truth?"

Leverette thought for a second.

"Does your gut tell you anything?" Leverette asked calming down a little.

"No." Marsden said and looked through the window at Carole.

"I don't think she's lying about seeing the murder," Leverette said looking through the window now. "I just don't know if she's not part of it. What about Ms. Lang?"

"I don't think she had anything to do with it," Marsden said, "Once she started talking about the dream, I didn't have that feeling she was hiding something anymore."

"And you don't believe in this 'nonsense'," Leverette

said and turned back to him. "You've a touch of it yourself."

"Bull shit," Marsden said and went to open the door.

Carole looked up at the two men, waiting to see if she was going to be locked up.

"Ms. Sage, you and Ms. Lang can leave now," Leverette said with that grin.

"Just stay in town in case we have more questions," Marsden added shaking his head at his partner's infatuation.

"Okay, thank you," Carole said and got up and left the room. As she walked past Leverette, she had a funny feeling but she didn't know what it was about, so she kept it to herself.

Chapter Seventeen

KEN DENTON WAS SCHEDULED NEXT. He called to say that he would be a little late so that had given Leverette and Marsden enough time to talk to Carole Sage.

Leverette couldn't get her off his mind. He hoped they'd end this case soon so he could ask her out. If they hadn't interviewed her and he'd just met her he could have. *Damn!*

The desk sergeant called Marsden to let him know Denton was there. He went out to get him while Leverette sat and waited.

When Denton and Marsden walked in, Leverette watched as Marsden pointed to the chair for him to sit.

"I don't know what else I can tell you that I didn't tell you yesterday," Denton said.

"Sometimes when people get a chance to sleep on it,

they remember things," Leverette said with an 'I mean business' attitude.

"Sleep on it? You think I was able to sleep on it?" Denton yelled. "I didn't get any sleep last night. I don't think I'll ever sleep again!"

Marsden and Leverette looked at each other. Ms. Lang said the same thing.

"We understand finding the leg like you did is a bit traumatic," Marsden started to say.

"A bit traumatic? You think it was just a bit traumatic?" Denton yelled again. "It's not something you come across on a normal day."

"Calm down, Mr. Denton. We don't want you to have another heart attack," Marsden said in his soothing voice.

Denton looked down at the tabletop and took a breath.

"You're probably going to think I'm crazy," he started then looked up at each of the detectives. "I dreamt about that leg."

"What did you dream?" Leverette asked.

Denton looked at Leverette to see if he was mocking him. He wasn't.

"I saw this man, I think it was a man anyway, dressed like a surgeon. I've seen my share of them over the years. There was a woman lying on a table cut into pieces. He picked up her right leg and put it into a black garbage bag, looked me right in the eyes and shushed me."

Marsden was making notes as Denton spoke.

"Did you recognize anything?"

Denton thought for a bit and said, "No. Couldn't see the lady's face or his. Just his eyes."

"What about the room?" Marsden asked.

"Just a room. Didn't look too big and only had one light hanging."

Marsden and Leverette exchanged glances.

"Why? What's up?"

"Nothing," Marsden said.

"You think I'm nuts, then."

"No," Leverette said. "We have open minds when it comes to insight."

"Oh," Denton said. "Can I go now? I don't have anything more to tell you. Oh, I just remembered; after he looked at me, I heard an owl hoot three times."

"Okay, you can leave just stay close to home," Marsden said, "In case we need to talk to you again."

"Not a problem," Denton said and stood up.

The detectives stood and Leverette opened the door.

"Have a nice day," Leverette said.

"Yeah, right," Denton said.

The detectives sat at the table and faced each other.

"That makes two who had dreams, and one who had a similar vision," Marsden said looking at his notes. "You believe in this crap, what do you think?"

"Hard to say," Leverette said and sat back in his chair thinking a minute.

The rest of the interviews went the same with only one who didn't say anything about a dream. Shin Yoo. He seemed a little nervous and this sent up red flags for the two detectives.

"I told you," he said to the detectives, "I haven't been to the house since my father's death."

"Your sister was, though," Leverette said, "And she could have placed the left arm there for you to find."

"My sister could never do such a thing," Yoo said.

"What makes you think so?" Marsden asked.

"She is just not the type of person to do this."

"We might have to call her in for an interview," Leverette said. "Unless you have a good reason for us not to."

Yoo sat back in his chair and shook his head. "She's in a wheelchair from a car accident three years ago. She is paralyzed from the waist down."

"So, she needs someone to drive her around?" Marsden asked.

"No. She has a modified van that she learned to drive," Yoo said. "But if she has to drive a long distance, her husband drives."

"Okay, Mr. Yoo," Marsden said, "Don't leave town." He handed his card to Yoo. "If you think of anything, please feel free to call."

"Yeah," was all he said.

The detectives got out and let Yoo precede them on the way out.

Once he was out of ear shot Marsden said, "Have you heard back from Gordon yet?"

"Gordon said there was no connection with any of the

people who found a body part. He did say the body was that of a Heather North. Did he find anything out about Ms. Sage?"

"I haven't heard yet," Leverette said and took his phone out. "I'll give him a call."

He dialed as the two walked over to their desks.

"Gordon, Leverette here. Did you find out anything about Heather North or Carole Sage?"

"Let me see here," Gordon said, and Leverette could hear him shuffling some papers. "Looks like Ms. North went through a nasty divorce last year. Ms. Sage is clean. Nothing. Not even a parking ticket."

"Do you have Ms. North's husband's name and info?"

"Yeah, Arthur North, 670 Gratiot, Marysville, phone is 810-364-9878. Three sons and is remarried. That's it. He's a vet."

"A veterinarian?"

"No, Iraq. He works for a local building company now. Nimitz Brothers is the name; it's on Wadhams Road."

"Okay, thanks," Leverette said as he wrote everything down then hung up the phone.

"What's that all about?" Marsden asked noticing the look on Leverette's face.

"Gordon said she was in a nasty divorce," he said and looked at Marsden. "His name is Arthur North."

"He must not be in contact with her. Never called in a missing person," Marsden said.

"Gordon said they had three kids. Two with Heather

and one with his new wife, Charlene," Leverette said. "I'll call and set up a time for him to come in."

Arthur North got off work at 4 p.m. and headed directly to the police station.

Leverette showed him into the interrogation room and Marsden came in shortly after.

"All right," North began, "What's she saying I did this time?"

"What makes you think she said anything?" Marsden asked.

"Why else am I here then? She's always complaining about something and reporting me to you guys or her attorney or the counselor we see."

Marsden looked at North and studied him for a bit. North was on edge and looked really pissed.

"Are the boys with you?" Marsden asked.

"Yeah, I get them for one month in the summer. Why?"

"When was the last time you spoke to Heather?" Leverette asked and carefully watched North's reaction.

North's face went from angry to puzzled. "When I picked up the boys two weeks ago. Why?" He looked from Leverette to Marsden. "Is something wrong?"

"We're sorry to inform you but your ex-wife has been murdered," Marsden said in a soft voice still keeping an eye on North's reaction.

"What? I don't believe you," North said.

Leverette and Marsden had decided not to tell him what had happened to her.

"Do you know of anyone who would want to harm her?" Marsden asked.

"Besides me, no," North said. "But I didn't kill her. So, you guys are homicide?"

"Yes," Leverette said.

"Have the boys spoken to her since they were here with you?" Marsden asked.

"Sometimes. She's a real bitch when it comes to visitation."

"How's that?" Leverette asked this time.

North adjusted his posture in the seat. "When they finally get to see me, she talks to them on the phone for hours. That takes my time away from them. Or if one of the boys call her, she doesn't answer."

"Why wouldn't she answer? Doesn't she want to talk to them?" Leverette asked again.

"They aren't old enough to have their own phone, so they call on mine. She won't answer. And if they call on Charlene's phone, same thing."

Leverette didn't like his smart-ass attitude and it was starting to eat at him. Marsden noticed and took over the interview.

"When was the last time the boys spoke to her?"

"Let's see, today's Thursday, so I'd have to say Sunday."

"So, she doesn't call every day?" Marsden asked.

"Nope."

"So, she'll go days without speaking to them?" Marsden asked.

"Yup. And has everyone believe I'm stopping them from talking to each other."

"You did hear us say she's been murdered?" Leverette was trying to figure this guy out.

"Yes, I heard you. If you're waiting for me to cry, you're in for a long wait."

Leverette and Marsden looked at each other then back to him.

"Where were you Wednesday?" Leverette asked.

"I was with my boys all day," North said sounding defensive.

"Anyone, other than the boys, able to corroborate this?" Marsden asked.

"My wife, my neighbors, and the people at the pizza place I took them to for dinner."

"What about that evening?" Marsden asked.

"I was sleeping. My wife was with us all day and night." North was starting to get pissed. "I didn't kill her."

"Aren't you even curious as to how she died?" Marsden asked.

"Nope," North said.

His demeanor had the detectives stumped. He didn't care and had nothing much to say about his ex-wife's murder. Other than that, he didn't care.

The detectives thought for a minute then Marsden spoke.

"We'll notify her next of kin about this," he said, still watching North's reaction.

"Have at it," North said. "Are we done?"

"Yeah," Marsden said and started to get up.

"Don't bother, I know my way around here," North said as he got up. He walked to the door, opened it and left.

Leverette and Marsden sat there looking at each other trying to understand what just happened.

"All my years and I've never interviewed anyone like him," Leverette said.

"Well, we'll need to watch Yoo and North closely," Marsden said.

The two detectives left the interrogation room and headed to their desks.

Chapter Eighteen

WHEN THEY GOT to the squad room, they noticed a package on Leverette's desk. The box was a twenty inch, perfectly square box.

"You order something?" Marsden asked.

"No," Leverette said and examined the label on the box. "I don't recognize the return address either."

Instinctively, he pulled a pair of gloves from his desk and began to carefully open the box with his pocketknife. It cleared the scanner so there wasn't anything destructive in it.

Inside the box was a Styrofoam box that was cold to the touch. Something inside Leverette told him this wasn't going to be good.

Marsden also put on a pair of gloves and helped pull the Styrofoam box out. They both looked at each other.

"I think I want the chief here," Leverette said.

"I'll go get him," Marsden said and headed for the

chief's office. Within a matter of minutes Billingsley and Marsden were at Leverette's desk.

"What's this all about?" Billingsley asked.

"Don't know, Chief," Leverette said. "I just have a bad feeling about this."

"Okay, open it," Billingsley said, his curiosity building.

Carefully Leverette pulled the tape that was holding the top and bottom together.

The three men gasped as they saw a human head in the box.

"All right, don't touch anything. I'll get the lab here to take this and call the doc." Billingsley said.

Billingsley went into his office and stood behind his desk. He dialed the lab and waited and watched Leverette knowing all too well that he was going to look in the box. He watched as Leverette opened it and the reaction he had to its contents. When he finished the calls and wrote up the transfer of property, or TOP, papers he went back to Leverette's desk.

Leverette wanted to see if he knew who the head had belonged to. While Billingsley was in his office Leverette carefully tilted the head to see the whole face.

"Oh my god!" Leverette said as he gently tilted the head back to its original position.

"What?" Marsden asked. "Who is it?"

"Philip King," Leverette said and sat down heavily in his chair.

"The kid?" Marsden asked.

"Yup," was all Leverette could say.

"Who is it?" Billingsley asked, not really wanting to know.

"Philip King," Marsden said. "There's a note with it."

Since Billingsley didn't have any gloves on, he read over Marsden's shoulder. He let out a long whistle.

The note said, "You'll never catch me."

"That bastard," Billingsley said. "He's playing a game now."

"I wonder if we're going to find body parts all over the place again," Marsden said. They both looked at Leverette who just sat there staring. He felt like shit. "The poor kid," he thought.

Two men from the lab, Mark and Doug, came up to the desk from the elevator. They knew it was a small box but didn't want to handle it any more than they had to.

Doug took the TOP paper from Billingsley and signed the bottom of it, took his copy and handed the top sheet back to the chief.

Mark, in the meantime, carefully picked up the box and put it on the stretcher. He already had gloves on.

"Carrington will send the box to you once he removes its contents," Billingsley told them.

"No problem, Chief," Mark said. "We can pick it up from the morgue. Just let the doc know. If you guys are done, we'd like your gloves, too."

Marsden and Leverette carefully removed the gloves and placed them into the evidence bags they were handed.

"Okay," Billingsley said and turned to Leverette. "You gonna be okay, Joe?" he asked.

Leverette looked up at the chief with moist eyesand nodded.

"That son-of-a-bitch isn't going to get away with this," Leverette said through clenched teeth and pounded the top of his desk. "He was just a kid!" Leverette stood up just as Marcie walked up to his desk. His demeanor frightened her for a second and she decided not to flirt with him this time.

"I came for the,,," she stopped a second, "for the Styrofoam box."

Billingsley handed her the TOP paper and after she signed it, she put on a pair of gloves. Carefully, almost lovingly, she picked up the box and headed back to the elevator. Marsden followed to push the buttons for her.

"We're going to get him, Joe," Billingsley said and walked up to him. He placed his hand on Leverette's shoulder, but Leverette didn't feel it. He was lost in thought trying to figure out how he was going to stop this asshole.

"Do you think he's going to go through all the others?" Leverette asked in a low, angry voice.

"Hard to say, son," Billingsley said. "We'll have to get in touch with them all and see if they have some other place to stay until we catch him."

Leverette nodded thinking about Carole. If he touches her, he's going to regret the day he started all this shit."

Chapter Nineteen

DR. CARRINGTON LOOKED at the Styrofoam box sitting on his exam table. Marsden had called just before Marcie had brought it in to him, to let him know who it was.

Carrington put on his gloves and peeled the tape off and carefully placed it in an evidence bag. He knew the lab would want everything to examine.

Even though he knew who was in the box when he saw the young man's face, he couldn't help but draw in a long breath. He shook his head and placed it on the head stand that he placed right next to the box.

He started combing through the boy's hair to get any particulates for the lab. There were a few and he placed them in another evidence bag. Next, he turned to look at the face. The boy looked as if he were just sleeping. No sign that he knew what was happening. No terror.

When Carrington examined the rest of the head, he

didn't see any trauma, except for the part of the head that was severed from his body.

When he checked that out, he shook his head.

"Marcie, get Leverette down here," he called.

"Sure thing," she said and headed to the squad room. She hated the way this ate at Leverette. He was always trying to avoid her but now she was going to avoid him.

Leverette and Marcie walked into the doc's exam room. When he saw the head on the table it made his blood boil all the more. Marcie went back to what she was doing in the office.

"What'd you find, Doc?" Leverette asked.

Carrington sighed and looked directly in Leverette's eyes.

"Same saw blade was used on the boy," Carrington said and shook his head. "This weirdo is something else."

Leverette looked at the boy and thought he looked peaceful. Then his phone went off.

"Yeah," he said into it. "Shit! I'll be right up."

The doc looked at him wondering what was going on.

"They found the body," Leverette said. "Looks like he was killed in his own bed."

"What a fucking mess," Carrington said to no one in particular. He turned back to the boy and finished getting samples before he got ready to go to the crime scene.

Marsden informed Leverette about the boy's body as they drove to the King's home.

"Mr. King left for work around 5 a.m., the Mrs. left just after 7 a.m. Neither checked on Phil before they left, stating that he got up around 7:30 a.m. to get ready for school.

"Since Phil had never missed a day of school in his life, the principal called Mrs. King to let her know he never showed up. This was around 9 a.m.; school starts at 8:30.

"Mrs. King was able to leave work to go check on him. Her boss knew about what had happened last week and agreed to let her go.

"When she got home, she noticed his books still on the dining room table and called out to him. She said she listened for the shower, wondering if he just slept too long but got no answer. She said she had an uncomfortable feeling when she was there and was almost afraid to go upstairs to check his bedroom. Mrs. King was considering about calling her husband but if he just overslept it would be a waste of time, so she headed upstairs."

"His door was closed, and she noticed an odd odor coming from his room. It smelled like copper," with that, Marsden had to stop and gather himself, then he continued. "When she opened the door, all she saw was the blood on the pillow and she turned and ran."

"She didn't go in to check on him?" Leverette asked as they turned into the King's driveway.

"No. She said she saw his head was gone and the smell was horrible. When she got downstairs it took her a bit to gather herself together and call her husband, then the police."

"First officer was on the scene within fourteen minutes, checked the house then went to check the boy.

"He called Billingsley, who in turn called the CSIs and then he wanted us. I told him you were with Carrington and he had me call you immediately," Marsden finished as they parked the car and got out.

He saw the King's holding each other on the front porch of their colonial style home, crying into each other's shoulders. He hated this shit and wondered if he or Billingsley should have called Mr. King when the package arrived at the station. Too late now.

The detectives walked up to the porch and offered their condolences to the couple. The King's pulled themselves together and thanked them.

"We *will* find out who did this to Phil," Leverette promised.

Marsden nodded his head, and they went into the home.

The first responding officer was there at the door. He was a young man, maybe in his twenties. His sharp blue eyes had a steely gaze coming from under his hat.

"Were you the first responder?" Marsden asked, as Leverette was too pissed off to speak just yet and decided to have a look around the house.

"Yes, sir," the officer said. "When I arrived, Mrs. King was standing on the porch and did not want to go in to sit down. She proceeded to tell me when she got home and went to her son's bedroom all she saw was blood and smelled an awful stench."

"Thank you, Marks," Marsden said looking at the name on the officer's jacket.

He looked up to Leverette standing at the bottom of the stairs looking as if he was debating about ascending them. Marsden walked over.

"Ready to go up?" Marsden asked.

"Yeah, but first I want to talk to Betty," Leverette said.

Betty was an exceptionally gorgeous woman. Her long auburn hair and large green eyes made every man in the station pine for her. She had curves that would make any model cringe and a soft sexy voice, legs that went to heaven. Leverette was the only man not affected by her charms and nobody understood why.

He walked up to her as she was examining the furniture.

"Hey Betty," Leverette said.

She turned and looked him directly in the eye. They were the same height. "Hi Joe," she said, the sadness in her eyes and her voice evident. "I hate when this shit happens to kids."

Leverette nodded. "Me, too. Have you checked outside yet?"

"Yes, I have two of my people out there right now. They're paying particular attention to the spot under his window," she told him as she pointed to the window. "I haven't heard from them yet. I was just getting ready to go upstairs when I noticed this chair was moved." She looked down at the depressions in the carpet and Leverette followed her gaze.

"Maybe Mrs. King moved it when she ran from the house?" he said.

"That wouldn't really make sense. The stairwell comes down there, and the door to the porch is directly across from it. Why would she come ten feet this way just to get outside?"

"Good point, Betty, I'll have to ask her," he said and headed for the stairs where Marsden waited. Betty was right behind him.

As they topped the stairs the pungent odor became evident. When they entered the room one man was taking pictures while the other was looking around the room, especially checking the window area.

Marsden couldn't bring himself to get too close to the body, while Leverette and Betty walked right up to the bed.

They noticed there were some tears in the pillow and a note taped to the headboard.

"He was decapitated while he slept," Betty said as she examined the pillow. She took down the note and noticed it had Leverette's name on it.

"Here," she said and handed him a pair of gloves. "Put these on and see what that asshole has to say."

Leverette took the gloves and put them on, then carefully opened the envelope and took out the note.

Betty noticed his face turn a bright red and then saw the anger in his eyes. A look she had seen on many occasions.

"What's it say?" Marsden asked, still keeping a safe distance.

"Six to go," Leverette said. "The last will be your lady love."

Everyone stopped what they were doing because it was well known, that since his family was killed, he had never expressed a desire to date. They all turned to him with surprised looks on their faces.

Betty noticed. "Get back to work everyone," she said and watched until they all got back to their tasks.

Carrington arrived and wasn't too impressed with the fact he would have to climb the staircase to see the victim. He hadn't been feeling well all morning and now he wished he'd sent Smith to this one.

With a deep sigh, he started up the stairs. Once he got to the top, he dropped his bag and grabbed his left side. Leverette saw him and ran to him as the doctor slid down the wall.

Leverette turned to Betty, "He's having a heart-attack."

Betty ran over and unbuttoned his coat and Leverette helped her get it off . Then she got on the phone and called for an ambulance.

Carrington sat and winced with the pain but tried to stay calm knowing full well getting upset would just aggravate it. He'd seen plenty of people on his table who would still be alive if they just remained calm until help arrived.

"Smith," he managed to get out with much effort. Leverette knew he meant for him to call her to take over.

"Okay," Leverette said, and speed dialed the morgue.

"Morgue, Marcie here," he heard her say.

"Marcie, Dr. Carrington is having a heart-attack and requested that Dr. Smith come to the scene."

"Oh my God!" Marcie screamed into the phone. "He didn't look so good this morning. I'll get her right over. Is he okay?"

"Seems like he'll be. You have the address?"

"Yes. Have you called an ambulance? Of course you did. Never mind. I'll tell her right away. Let us know what you can about George."

Leverette was taken aback by her informality but let it go. He figured they'd worked side-by-side for quite some time and he probably had his staff call him by his first name.

"Sure. I'll give them the number to the office," Leverette said and hung up.

He turned to Carrington. "Dr. Smith is on her way."

Carrington nodded his head and just sat back. Leverette worried about his friend but knew he had to get back to work.

Betty sensing this said, "Go, I'll stay with him until the paramedics arrive."

Leverette nodded his head and went back into the bedroom. Marsden was looking through his computer and checking out his desk.

"Was that note handwritten?" he asked Leverette.

"Yeah. See if you can find any paper and envelopes that look like these," he handed Marsden the letter and envelope, which he had since put in an evidence bag. Marsden took it and went back to the desk checking the papers on the top, then going through the drawers.

A siren screamed in the front of the house and frightened the Kings. They had no idea the coroner had a heart-attack.

Leverette came down the stairs to let them know where they were needed. They nodded and headed into the house and up the stairs.

He turned to the Kings. "Our coroner had a heart-attack."

They looked at him and shook their heads.

"I need to ask if either of you moved the chair in the front room."

They looked at each other than at him with a puzzled look on their faces.

"Come with me and I'll show you the one I mean," he said and let them go into the house first. "This one," he said pointing to a wing-back chair.

"No, I didn't move it. Did you?" Mrs. King asked her husband.

"No. Had no reason to," he answered. "Why?"

"Just needed to know," was all he'd tell her. Leverette suspected from the way the chair was turned that the killer had sat in it in the dark out of view of the two parents as they got ready for work.

"We'll need your statements," he told them. "Perhaps

you'd rather go to the station to give them while we finish the investigation here. The officer will take you, but you'll have to find a place to stay for a while."

"Sure," Mr. King said. "Can we grab some things first?"

"Yeah, no problem," Leverette said.

As they pulled out of the driveway Leverette called Billingsley.

"Hey Chief, a bit of a problem but it's taken care of," Leverette said. "Before I get to it, I sent the Kings to the station. One of the officers is bringing them. I didn't want them here when they brought their boy down."

"Good thinking, Joe," Billingsley said. "They don't need to see Carrington bringing the body down."

"Well, he wouldn't be, Chief. He had a heart-attack when he got here."

"What? Who's coming down then?"

"Dr. Smith. She just pulled up," Leverette said as he saw her pull into the driveway. He was holding the door open for the paramedics.

"Okay. Is anyone with Carrington?"

"It looks like Barb is here with the doc."

"Good. I'll take care of the Kings. Keep me posted on Carrington, too."

"No problem, Chief," Leverette said and hung up. He stayed by the door for Smith and Barb and brought them up to date with what they'd found so far.

"So, Carrington never saw the body?" Dr. Smith asked. She was a handsome woman, maybe in her fifties , and had hardened eyes. Leverette thought this was because of her work.

"No, he'd just made it up the stairs when it hit," Leverette said. "He told me to call you."

"I've told that jerk to lose weight. He thought quitting smoking would be enough. You'd think after all the years in our line of work he'd know better," Smith said gruffly and headed into the bedroom where she saw the other investigators.

The CSI team didn't care for Smith, and neither did Marsden. She didn't come across as a nice lady and never smiled. At least Carrington was known to smile at times; even laugh.

Betty turned and looked at Smith. "We only took pictures. Nobody touched the body."

"Good," was all Smith said and started the examination, while Barb looked around the room, then under the bed. When Smith pulled the cover back Barb stood up and helped her turn the body. One thing about Smith: she was thorough. Even though the cause of death was so obvious she had to check everything. They put the body down and Smith's eye caught something.

"Give me the magnifying glass," she barked at Barb.

Barb didn't let it bother her, she'd worked with Smith for twenty some years and realized that's just Smith. She reached into the tote and pulled out the magnifying glass and handed it to her. Smith concentrated on a section on the boy's upper arm.

"This is fresh," she said to Barb who made her way to that side of the bed. "Look."

Barb took the glass and examined the puncture wound. "I see it," she said.

"Unless this young man received this from a doctor this will show the same as it did for that woman," she said sounding so heartless that the CSIs in the room swallowed hard.

"Alright, let's get him to the morgue," Smith said, and Barb pulled out the transport bag from her tote. She unzipped it and while Smith rolled the body to one side and. Barb held him and Smith slid the bag under. Then they put him on the stretcher they'd carried up and packed their tools.

Leverette came back up as they were getting ready to leave.

"Are the parents around?" Smith asked.

"No," was all Leverette said.

"Okay. Let's go," she said to Barb and the two started down the steps and out the door.

The CSI now gathered up the bedding and pillows and placed them in separate evidence bags, along with prints and other items that might help identify the murderer. They headed out, also.

"Can't find that type of paper anywhere," Marsden said to Leverette. "He must have written it before he got here."

"Smug son-of-a-bitch," Leverette said, "What if this didn't work out for him?"

Marsden knew he didn't want an answer and just shook his head.

When they headed to the family room Betty and a couple of her people were gathering evidence from the moved chair.

"Joe, you have to see this," Betty called when she saw him. Both detectives made their way over.

Betty was holding a magnifying glass over one arm of the chair. "We almost missed this."

She handed the glass to Leverette and he tried to see what she saw. He looked for a while and didn't see anything.

"We didn't see it at first," Betty said, "Then something caught Glen's eye and he looked closer. It says 'HA HA HA' if you look close enough."

Leverette looked again and there it was. Spelled out in what looked like string or hair.

"I'll get on this right away. Nothing else on this chair though," Betty said.

He handed the magnifying glass to Marsden and pointed to where the words were. "Damn," Marsden said. "What if we didn't find this? And just what the hell is he trying to prove?"

"Have no fucking idea," Leverette said and stormed out of the house.

Chapter Twenty

WHEN LEVERETTE and Marsden got back to the station Billingsley waved them into his office. He noticed Leverette's mood and wondered what else had gone wrong.

"Okay, what's up?" he asked the two detectives.

"That bastard left two messages. One was a count down with Carole Sage being the last. The other was odd," Leverette said deciding to sit down. "He had 'HA HA HA' spelled out in string on the chair he waited in."

Billingsley sat back in his chair and looked from Leverette to Marsden and shook his head.

"This is the worst crime this city has ever seen," Billingsley said. "Anything from the initial investigation?"

"No, no prints. No sign of forced entry," Marsden said. "Betty's going to get back to us about that thread, and Smith thinks he was injected with the same drug Heather North was."

Leverette leaned forward with his elbows on his knees and head in his hands. "What the hell is going on? Why is he killing these witnesses? They never saw him!" He looked up at Billingsley. The anger evident in his eyes.

"Gordon might be able to give us a better idea of the guy," Billingsley said to them both.

"If he's going after the witnesses, we should warn them," Marsden said and pulled out his note pad. "If he's going backward then Frank McCullough will be next."

"That poor guy's scared out of his mind as it is. If we say something to him, he's likely to lose it completely," Leverette said looking over to Marsden.

"Have either of you talked to him?"

"No. He wouldn't even come in for the interview we did just after," Marsden told him. "He's holed up good and tight. Might even be safe where he is."

"What I want to know is how the fuck he knows who the witnesses are?" Leverette said and sat up. "The press doesn't even know about this case." He slammed his fists on the chairs' arms. "Do we have a leak?"

"The press doesn't even know about the crime yet. I have no idea, Joe," Billingsley said leaning forward and resting his arms on his desk. "We've kept this quiet."

"So, there's a chance he doesn't know who else is on our witness list," Marsden said.

"Bullshit!" Leverette said. "What about that message he left at the Kings? Six to go, the last my lady love?"

Marsden and Billingsley looked at each other knowing how he acted around Ms. Sage. They had chuckled about it after her interview, out of Leverette's earshot. It was just that obvious.

"How does he know anything other than the murder?" Leverette spat. . "We were on a different radio frequency so the scanners wouldn't pick it up."

"He could have searched or had several scanners set up until he got the names," Marsden said, then he thought a minute. "How did he know about Ms. Sage? Her name was never mentioned."

"This whole case is baffling. Why Heather North? Why Philip King? Is McCullough going to be next?" Leverette asked looking at the two of them. "Or is he going at random?"

"Type up the report and I'll send it over to Gordon. He might have some idea about who we're looking for," Billingsley told them. "They put a rush on the autopsies and lab work. Hopefully, we'll get some answers to help with the case soon."

They got up and headed to their desks. Leverette turned on his computer and searched through his messages. He had one from the lab and decided to go there to talk to them.

"I'll be back in a bit," he told Marsden. "I'm going to the lab," and he got up and headed for the elevator.

When he got to the lab, Mark and Doug were looking something up on the computer. Mark looked up when he saw Leverette.

"Hey," he said and went back to what they were looking at.

"Hi," Leverette said. "Got anything on my case?"

Mark pushed away from the desk and got up. He picked up a folder and handed it to Leverette.

"The victims were both injected with Xylazine. The North woman didn't get as much as the King boy, though."

Leverette looked through the folder he was handed and closed it.

"What's zylain?" he asked.

"Xylazine. It's a horse tranquilizer. Not as common around here as Ketamine, though. If given to a person. they drift in and out of consciousness. A larger dose has been known to be used in suicide attempts. We think he killed the boy before decapitating him, but we won't be sure until Carrington finishes with the autopsy."

"Dr. Smith is doing the autopsy. Carrington is in the hospital. Heart attack."

"He gonna be okay?" Doug asked as he turned to face them.

"Yeah, he just needs to lose a bit of weight and he'll be better than new."

"That's good. We sent a copy to the morgue so, as I said, once they finish, they'll have more for you," Mark said.

"Good. Have you checked with the local vets to see if any of them ordered this other tranquilizer?" Leverette asked already forgetting how to pronounce its name.

"That's what we're working on now. Only two labs make it and we're checking on who in our area ordered it. That way if one of them is our killer he won't get spooked," Doug said.

"Send me what you find, guys," Leverette said and turned to leave the lab.

He thought about stopping by the morgue but then Smith really hadn't had time to do much, maybe just to start the autopsy. Leverette decided to go talk to Gordon.

When he got to the elevator, he pressed the fourth floor. Gordon didn't have any more than they did, but maybe he knew something.

Gordon was sitting at his desk reading through some paperwork when Leverette walked in.

"Hey, Joe," he said and motioned for Leverette to sit.

"No thanks," Leverette said, "Only have a second. Wanted to know if there's anything new on this end."

Gordon sat back in his chair, took off his glasses and rubbed his nose ridge.

"I wish I could tell you more, Joe," he said, "But I don't have much more to go on. If you guys find something else out give me a holler."

"You heard about the King kid?"

"Yeah, that just confirms what I thought earlier. Well organized, thorough, works alone, sadistic, probably knew the first victim personally and is both seeking retribution for the witnesses reporting their findings, even though he or she wanted them found, and also having fun taunting you guys."

"I could have told you that," Leverette said, "Well the last part anyway. I'll keep you posted if anything else comes up."

"Okay," Gordon said, going back to reading his paperwork.

Leverette decided to return to his desk and see if Marsden had found out anything else.

Carole awoke that morning to the smell of bacon, eggs, and coffee. Since all of this began, Amy had been staying with her, which was fine. She was getting spoiled having breakfast ready every morning. She smiled to herself. Put on her robe and headed downstairs. And she loved having Bud around for protection.

"Morning," Amy said as she was setting the table. She noticed Carole was not dressed yet.

"Morning," Carole said and sat at her place. She reached down and scratched Bud behind his ears. He looked up at her and nuzzled her for more.

Amy went to the fridge to get the milk, butter, jam, and orange juice. Carole sat there wondering what was going on. The case the detectives were working on had something to do with her. But what?

"What's on your mind?" Amy asked, noticing Carole in deep thought.

"Oh, nothing really," Carole said. "Just wondering how I'm tied into this case."

"Did you have another one of your - thingys?"

Amy brought the platter of food to the table.

"Visions. No. I hope I don't," Carole said as she

poured the juice in her glass then took two pieces of toast to butter. "I wonder if those two detectives think I'm involved in some way."

"Now why would they think that?"

"Because I told them about my visions. How I saw that woman being cut up."

"If you were hiding something you wouldn't have said anything," Amy said taking the jam and spreading it on her toast. "Besides, when I talked to them, I told them you could sense things and that's why I wanted you to come with me."

Carole took a sip of her coffee and bite of toast. She wondered if she should call the detectives or just leave it be.

"Yeah, you're right. Of course, you're right. I'm not involved with this maniac!"

They looked at each other and chuckled.

When Amy left for work Carole loaded the dishes in the dishwasher and decided to take a long hot soak in her tub.

As the tub filled and she poured her bubble bath in she thought about the vision she had yesterday. She didn't want to tell Amy because it would just upset her.

Carole slid into the tub enjoying the warmth that started releasing the tension she was feeling. Maybe she'd go talk with the detectives. She couldn't remember their names but had one of their cards in her wallet. They needed to know about her latest vision, that is, if they even believed her.

Carole stayed in the tub until she felt better. It wasn't one hundred percent, but it was better than she was feeling when she got up this morning.

She dressed in a comfortable jogging outfit, not that she ever jogged, they were just so comfortable. She put her slippers back on and headed downstairs. Amy had put the paper on the kitchen table before she left so Carole decided on another cup of coffee and sat down to see what was in the local news.

The detectives made it clear they didn't want the press in on anything, so she was surprised to see an article about human body parts being found in the area. The article went on to say that the police are not releasing any information at this time but would when they had more.

Damn, I wonder if the detectives saw this this morning. Then she ran upstairs to change; she was going to the police station to talk to them.

Before she went in, she pulled the business card to see what the detectives name was. Marsden. Okay, she didn't want to look like a fool when she went in.

At the desk she asked for him by name. The desk sergeant told her to wait a moment. The sergeant called up to Billingsley and he said he'd be right down. If Leverette or Marsden weren't in the building, they were to contact Billingsley about any visitors.

"It'll just be a second," the sergeant said, "You can have a seat."

Carole sat down and waited but the man approaching her wasn't Marsden or the other one.

"Ms. Sage, I'm Chief Billingsley, how may I help you?" he said with a pleasant face. He knew who she was and wondered if she'd seen something else.

"I was hoping to talk to Detective Marsden or his partner," she said standing and shaking his hand.

"He and Leverette are out on a case right now. Would you like to come to my office and tell me what you need?"

Carole thought a moment. "Sure," she said and followed him to his office.

When she walked past their desks, she got an eerie feeling. She didn't know they were their desks, but something nasty was going on with them at the moment.

Once in the office, Billingsley motioned to a seat and she sat down.

"Would you like some coffee?" he asked.

"No, thank you."

"Now what brings you here today?"

She didn't know how much he knew about her. He noticed her hesitation.

"Ms. Sage, I know you have had feelings or whatever you call them. Is that why you're here?"

She felt relieved and took a deep breath.

"They're visions, sir," she said. "I had another last night."

Billingsley sat back in his chair and looked her in the eyes. He nodded his head and said, "Go on."

"Well, it was a bit different from the other ones. I saw the same man, but he was dressed in black. He was holding someone's head by the hair, looked right into my eyes, and said 'shh'. Then an owl hooted. I looked at my clock and it was midnight."

Billingsley sat forward quickly. "You saw this at midnight?"

"Yes."

"And you don't recognize the face of the victim?"

"No, I've never seen him before," she answered wondering what he was getting at.

"But you could tell it was a male?"

"Yes. He looked young." She was getting nervous and wondered if she should say anything about the article in the paper. It wasn't on the first page so maybe nobody saw it.

The phone on Billingsley desk rang and it make Carole jump.

"Excuse me, please. Billingsley here," he said. "Good. I'll take care of the Kings. Keep me posted on Carrington, too." He hung up the phone and looked at Carole.

"Another thing," she said, "did you know that the murder is in the paper?"

With everything that happened this morning, Billingsley hadn't had a chance to look through it.

"No. Damn! Who the hell would have leaked it?" He looked at Carole and said, "If you could come back in about an hour or two, Leverette and Marsden will be back. Right now, I have another case."

"Yeah, sure. I'm not working today," she said and got up and left.

"Fuck," Billingsley said under his breath.

Chapter Twenty-One

CAROLE SAGE RETURNED to the precinct about an hour later. She walked to the front desk and told the sergeant she was here to see Billingsley.

The desk sergeant called to Billingsley and he said he'd be right there. On his way, he passed Leverette and Marsden's desks and told them to be in his office in five minutes.

"Sure, Chief," Marsden said. "What's up?"

"The Sage woman is here. I'm going to get her," Billingsley said and headed to the front desk.

"Ms. Sage," he said with a smile. "We're all ready to talk with you."

She smiled back and nodded her head then followed him to his office.

Leverette and Marsden, who were seated, stood when they entered. Billingsley noticed Leverette was trying to hide a smile. He had Carole sit at the opposite side of his desk that the detectives were on. He knew something was up and hoped Leverette wasn't going to blow the investigation with this attraction. He shook his head and sat behind the desk. He knew it would be good for Leverette to start seeing someone again but not now. Not her.

Leverette tried to adjust his chair so he could see her and bumped Marsden. "Sorry," he said. Marsden just rolled his eyes and looked at the chief. Both shook their heads.

"Okay, first thing, someone leaked the North murder to the paper. There was a short article in this morning's paper and I'm sure none of you had anything to do with it," Billingsley said looking at all of them in turn.

They shook their heads and he decided to continue.

"Obviously, they haven't been able to find out anything about the case so that's good. It almost reads as though they think it's a prank."

"The murderer could have sent something or called something in," Marsden said. I didn't get any calls from the press."

"I didn't either," Leverette said.

"Well, I'm checking with PR to see if they got anything. It wasn't first page so it's hard to say."

"Second, Ms. Sage said something this morning that I think is vital to these cases," Billingsley said turning to Carole. "Do you want to tell them about the vision you had last night?"

Leverette was pissed that he'd missed her this morning. What a great way to start his day.

"What I saw was the murderer, dressed in black with his face covered except for his eyes. He was holding a head by the hair then put his fingers to his lips and shushed me. I heard an owl hoot and when I looked at my clock it was midnight," she said feeling like she was in a dream or some other reality.

"Did you recognize the person?" Marsden asked.

"No, but he was young," she said. "I've never seen him before."

Marsden sat back in his chair and folded his arms across his chest. He stared at the front of the desk deep in thought. Billingsley was surprised Leverette didn't have anything to say. It was as if he were distracted and Billingsley didn't like that from his best detective.

To his surprise, Leverette spoke first.

"None of the witnesses know each other from what we've learned so far. What if we showed her their photos in case it happens again?"

That made Billingsley feel better; at least Leverette was thinking about the case.

"Especially since we don't know if he's going in any specific order, or if he's even going to keep going," Marsden said before looking up at Billingsley.

"I have a feeling he's not going to stop," Leverette said. "Should we say something to the other witnesses?"

"I think all that would do would cause them to panic. The only thing I can think of is to have Ms. Sage call one of you if she has another vision," Billingsley said. "If she saw this one, she might see the next one and we could catch him in the act."

Carole sat there not knowing if she wanted to be part of this. She knew there was a connection, but this was wearing on her.

"You live alone, Ms. Sage?" Marsden asked.

"Yes, for the most part. Amy Lang is staying with me since all this happened," Carole said and felt a chill go through her. What if he came for Amy at her house? Could she handle finding her body with a body part missing?

"Well according to the note, he's not coming for Ms. Sage until last," Leverette blurted out.

The Chief and Marsden glared at him and Carole stood up, shocked.

"Note? What note?" she asked and started shaking . Billingsley got up and went to her, gently putting his arm around her shoulder.

"Now, Ms. Sage, we're hoping to catch him before he gets to another person. With your help we will," he tried to sound reassuring.

He got her sit back down and poured her a cup of coffee. She took it and sipped at it, still in shock. She leaned back in her chair and stared into space.

Marsden looked at her and hoped she'd be able to hold on. He could just imagine the stress she was going through.

Once Carole had gotten herself together as best she could, Billingsley continued.

"It seems, for some reason, that these visions happened at midnight," he said, "and the murders happened sometime later, so we might be able to get him."

Leverette thought for a moment and nodded. "I could stay with her and when she lets me know I can call it in. That way we'll know Ms. Sage and Ms. Lang are safe, also."

Marsden raised his eyebrows, which was not wasted on Billingsley.

Billingsley thought for a moment and said, "I think we can have Gentry and Williams stay with her." He knew Leverette wouldn't like the idea, but two female officers would be better than one male officer, especially since he obviously had feelings for her.

Marsden didn't have to look at Leverette to know he was disappointed. He could almost feel the tension in him when Billingsley told him his plans.

"I'll be calling their captain and letting him know I want his officers to follow Ms. Sage home," Billingsley said and looked over at Carole.

"Okay," she said. "Amy will be there, with her dog, but I have a three-bedroom ranch so if one wants to sleep while the other is awake that won't be a problem."

"I think I'd like both of them to be awake, Ms. Sage. I'd feel safer," Billingsley said to her. "You two get what you needed from the lab?"

"I was getting ready to head to the morgue to see about, uh, to see if they have any more information," Leverette said almost slipping again. He knew Billingsley didn't want to get Carole any more freaked out than she already was.

"The lab is still working on the evidence from the King's home," Marsden said. "They'll let us know for sure once they find out."

"Okay, then you two get going and I'll take care of Ms. Sage," Billingsley said in a way that let them know it wasn't up for discussion.

Leverette looked at him wondering if he could tell he had feelings for her. *Shit, he must, if that damn murderer knows.* That thought made him wonder if it was someone on the force.

As they left the chief's office, they nodded at Carole, who gave them a forced smile. She was scared shitless now. A note. Why didn't Billingsley say anything about it? Was he trying to protect her?

Billingsley dialed the phone and asked about the two officers and explained why he needed them tonight. "Okay, Williams and Michaels then. Thanks, Paul. Have them report to me and I'll fill them in. I hope they have open minds."

After hanging up the phone he turned to Carole. "He'll call them and then I'll let them know what's up. I'll call you when they're on their way to your home."

"Can I ask you a question?" she asked coyly.

He knew what it was going to be about, and he made a mental note to kick Leverette's ass. "Sure."

She cleared her throat and squirmed in her seat. "Just what was on that note?"

Billingsley hung his head. He really didn't want to tell her but now he figured he had to. He opened the file that was right on top of the others on his desk.

"It said 'Six to go. The last will be your lady love,'" he looked up at her. "That's all it said."

"So, one of them is seeing one of the witnesses?" Carole asked. "That must be horrible for them."

She didn't notice Leverette's behavior. Marsden said he was grinning at her the whole time they spoke to her and not saying much. He decided to play it smart.

"Yes, it must be," was all he said. He got up and escorted her to the front of the precinct. "I'll call you as soon as I hear from the officers."

"Thank you," she said and left.

Chapter Twenty-Two

BILLINGSLEY CALLED Carole at 6 p.m. and told her the two officers would be there shortly. He clued them in to what was going on.

"Now, I know this is going to sound crazy," Billingsley started as the two women sat in his office. "The lady you're going to see is a sensitive." He stopped and waited for their reaction.

Williams' big brown doe eyes opened wide and Michaels raised an eyebrow. He wondered if this was going to work. He didn't know much about them but then Paul did know about the case and said they'd be the best.

Williams squirmed in her chair. Her chocolate brown skin looked smooth and she wore her hair short. Billingsley thought she was the most beautiful woman he'd ever seen. She reminded him of his late wife at that age. Their marriage was frowned upon, his family being white. But once the grandchildren came all was forgotten. Damn how he missed her.

Michaels on the other hand was light skinned, had green eyes that pierced right through you. Her hair was dyed blonde and short. She wasn't near as attractive as Williams, but she was a beauty in her own right.

Billingsley went over the case with them and asked if they had any questions. They both shook their heads, so he handed Michaels a paper with the address.

"I want you to stay there until I call you to come back," he said. "We're not sure what, if anything, will happen tonight. But if this guy is planning something, we're pretty sure it'll be tonight."

"Yes, sir," they both said. He dismissed them and they left for their assignment.

Amy called Carole to let her know she would be late. "It's been a madhouse here today," Amy told her, "I'll be a couple hours at least."

"Okay," Carole said, sounding subdued. "Dinner will be ready by seven." She didn't want to tell Amy about the officers until she got home. God knows she'd freak out.

"Great. See you then," Amy said and closed her phone. Carole sounded, what, tired? Worried? She decided to shrug it off and get back to work.

Williams and Michaels arrived at Carole's home at 6:12 p.m.. Carole welcomed them in, and they introduced themselves.

They sat in the living room and Carole brought out the coffee.

"So, you're a real sensitive?" Michelle Williams asked with interest.

Carole chuckled and looked at her. "I guess that's what they call it."

Barbara Michaels didn't believe in such things and it was evident on her face. "Do you see the future or what?" she asked.

"I see what's happening or going to happen," Carol answered.

"Wow," Michelle said. "That is so cool!"

Barbara shook her head and gave her one of her 'I don't believe you' looks. "You've seen the murders then?"

"Yes," Carole said, and a sad expression came over her face.

"Can you make that happen?" Barbara asked knowing if her boss believed it than it just might be true. And Billingsley seemed to believe it, too.

"No. They just come on their own," Carole said. "I've been able to see things since I was thirteen. This is the first time I've ever been involved with a police investigation."

The two officers nodded their heads and noticed headlights coming into the driveway. They got up and carefully went to the window.

"Oh, that's Amy," Carole said recognizing the car in the dimming light of the day. "She said she was going to be late."

The two officers heard her but didn't leave their spots. They kept an eye on her until she left the car, alone, and walked to the side door. They refused to relax until the woman was in the house and nobody was following her.

"Carole, who's ca…" she started to say and saw the two women in the house looking intently at her.

"These are Officers Williams and Michaels. They'll be here tonight…" Before she could finish Amy started to tremble.

"What? What happened? Is he coming here?" Amy started shuddering and barely made it into a chair at the kitchen table. Carole ran to her.

"No, he's not coming here," Carole said and went to get Amy a glass of water. She drank it slowly but couldn't stop shaking.

"This shit's going to kill me," Amy said. "I just don't understand."

"I know, sweetie, I know," Carole said and sat down across from her friend wondering the same thing.

The girls said good night to the two officers and went to bed. Carole had explained to Amy why they were there, but it didn't seem to calm her much. But Amy did admit that she felt safer with them there.

Williams and Michaels would check outside, through the windows since Carole had an alarm system.

The evening went by without incident until Carole ran into the living room.

"He's going to kill someone," she said shaking.

"Do you know who it will be?" Williams asked and led her to the sofa.

"No. Not this time," Carole's entire body was trembling.

"Didn't they show you the pictures of the others?" Michaels asked. "You should be able to recognize them."

"It's not like that," Carole said.

Amy came into the living room when she heard the commotion. She sat next to Carole and put an arm around her.

"It wasn't anyone in the pictures?" Michaels asked.

"I don't know," Carole said and started to cry. "He knows!"

"Get Billingsley over here," Michaels said to Williams. "Something's wrong."

Williams called and relayed the message while Michaels stayed with Carole and Amy. "Who was it then? Anyone you know?"

"I don't know," Carole said through sobs. She knew this person was going to die soon and she couldn't do anything to stop it.

Williams was at a loss. Was it someone she didn't know? No. She said she doesn't know, not she doesn't know them.

"He'll be here as soon as possible," Michaels said breaking Williams' chain of thought. "He wanted to know what was up. I told him we didn't know but that he should get here ASAP!"

"Good. Something's not right," Williams said looking at her partner.

Just then there was a knock at the door that made the

two officers get to their feet and put their hands on their weapons. Billingsley couldn't be there already; it took a good thirty-five minutes to get to Carole's house from the precinct.

Carefully, Williams moved to the front door to look through the pigeonhole. She shook her head and chuckled.

"It's Leverette," she said and unlocked the door. "Well, what brings you here at this time of night?" Williams teased. Billingsley told them he might show up and why.

Leverette's cheeks blushed and he thought for a minute.

"Just helping to keep an eye on the place," he said and came in. "I saw the lights come on. What's wrong?"

Williams led him into the living room and when he saw Carole crying, he had to fight the urge to wrap his arms around her, which Amy was doing already.

Leverette sat in the chair that was perpendicular to the sofa. His knee gently brushed against Carole's and she looked up at him.

"He knows," she said in a low whisper.

"Who knows? And what does he know?" Leverette asked taking his notepad and pen out of his pocket.

Carole had a lost look in her eyes. She sat back on the sofa and took a deep breath to try to steady herself.

"The killer," she said looking in Leverette's eyes. "He knows about me."

"What makes you think that?" Leverette asked already

making notes. He was wondering if she'd seen her head in his hands. "Did you see something?"

"Yes. His next victim. But the face was hidden," Carole said and started shaking again.

"Hidden?" Leverette asked.

"Blurred out. All I could tell is that it's a man with dark hair."

Leverette tried to think of who had dark hair that was on his list. King had dark brown hair, but he wasn't on the list anymore. Then there was DeShawn Davis, Shin Yoo and Frank McCullough.

"Could you tell anything about the hair? Long, short, curly…?"

Carole didn't want to remember what she saw, but this might help them stop the killer.

"It was straight and kind of long," she said as tears welled up in her eyes. "And I didn't see the killer's face, just his eyes, and he laughed instead of hushing me. Then I heard the owl, but it only hooted once."

A heavy knock on the door made everyone, except the two female officers, jump. Williams went to the door and peeked out. It was Billingsley. She let him in without saying anything. She pointed toward the living room.

He turned and wasn't surprised to see Leverette there.

"What's going on?" Billingsley asked in a gentle voice. He saw how upset Carole was and didn't want to add to it.

Leverette got up and motioned for Billingsley to follow him into the kitchen.

"She had the vision," Leverette said, "But the face was blurred out. She did see it was a man with longish dark hair."

"Can we figure out who it is?" Billingsley asked and mentally went through the faces of the witnesses.

"I think It's Frank McCullough," Leverette answered. "The other two with dark hair have short hair."

Billingsley got on the radio and ordered officers to McCullough's house. It was usually several hours after the vision and it was only 1 a.m. so they had time. He told them he and Leverette would meet them there.

The men walked back into the living room. Carole seemed to be calmed down a little but still had that look in her eyes.

"We think we know where he's going," Billingsley said, "So, we're heading out there. I want you two to stay here until we call."

"Yes, sir," they said in unison.

The men left and got into Billingsley's car then headed to McCullough's house.

Chapter Twenty-Three

THEY PULLED into McCullough's driveway and parked next to the patrol car. The house was a ranch style so they both thought the murderer could have gotten in with no problem.

The front door had been kicked in and one of the officers was outside vomiting.

"Shit!" Leverette said and jumped out of the car and ran to the porch. The officer who had gotten sick was wiping his mouth with his handkerchief. He looked up at Leverette and shook his head.

"We called the ME already and the Paramedics. He left one alive."

This threw Leverette. He left a witness? That made no sense. Billingsley was standing there when the officer gave the quick report.

"Let's go in," Billingsley said, and the two men pulled gloves from their pockets and put them on.

The lights were on and the second officer, Monroe, came into the living room.

"Talk to me," Billingsley said. The smell of death was in the air.

"When we got here, we rang the doorbell and got no answer. Greene went to check if the cars were here and he said a car and truck were parked in the garage. We put on our gloves and kicked in the door.

"We drew our weapons and walked in, but nobody was around. Well, not moving around.

"Greene turned on the light and we went through the rest of the house. They're in the bedroom."

Monroe led them to the bedroom, and they couldn't believe what they saw, Frank, minus the head, and his wife, Nancy. Blood saturated the pillow and spray was on the headboard and some had bounced back onto the blanket. The cut looked neat, just like the others.

Leverette walked up to Nancy and felt for a pulse. She was alive but out, and he hoped she'd stay that way for a while. She didn't need to see her husband like this.

The sound of sirens coming to the house made him feel better. Get her to the hospital and find out what he'd given her. He started taking a bunch of pictures because he knew Smith would have a fit that the crime scene was messed with.

When he called the morgue, he got the operator who said she'd call Smith.

A couple minutes went by and his phone rang.

"Leverette," he said.

"This is Smith, what's going on?"

"Another decapitation. Only this time we have a living lying next to the corpse. We're sending her to the hospital before she comes to. This isn't something she needs to wake up to."

"What?" Smith was livid. "Don't touch a thing until I get there," she said and hung up.

Heartless bitch.

Billingsley went to the door to let the paramedics know what to expect when they went in the bedroom.

"Is that why the officer got sick?" one of them asked Billingsley.

"Yes. And he's been on the force for twelve years," he said and led them down the hall to the bedroom.

"Whew!" one of them said. "That would be horrible to wake up next to." He went over to Nancy to check her vitals.

The other paramedic went to get the board and when he got back, they carefully placed her on it. They'd heard Leverette talking to Smith and were afraid they'd get written up for messing with a crime scene. Nancy was starting to stir, and they hurried her out to the rig.

Betty and her group showed up just as the paramedics were loading Nancy into their vehicle. The CSI team donned their gloves, grabbed their equipment, and headed in. They followed the voices down the hall and to the bedroom.

"Smith's not here yet?" Betty asked Leverette, "I'm

surprised, she usually flies over to a crime scene. Does she think she's CSI too?"

"I'm in hot water with her," Leverette said, "The wife was still alive, and we didn't want her waking up and seeing her husband like this."

"Oh boy, she's going to come in in a rage!" Betty said and chuckled. "She must be a hell of a good ME or she has something on them. I can't believe they put up with her."

"You don't know?" Leverette said raising his eyebrows.

"What?"

"Besides receiving accolades in her field she's the chief's nephew's wife."

"She doesn't look African American."

"She's not. I will tell you she does have beautiful kids," Leverette said.

"I wonder if they're like her?" Betty asked and chuckled. She walked to Frank's side of the bed and began examining the blood spray.

"Nothing was touched on this side?"

"No," Leverette said, "And they were very careful with the covers on this side. Nancy, his wife, had some splatter on her but it was minimal. I put the covers back like they were before they moved her.

"Yes, there's some on her pillow, too." Betty got her tablet out and started making notes, then got out her camera and started taking pictures using the measuring tools to indicate the size of some of the drops of blood.

"He must have held the head right over here for a second," Betty said pointing to the non-directional drops on the blanket. She looked at the floor but there were no drops. "I'll bet this is where he put Frank's head in the bag. See how this blood is in relation to the others?"

Leverette looked at the blanket and nodded. He liked Betty; she would explain the things she noticed if he was nearby.

They both jumped when Smith yelled, "I hope you didn't touch the body!"

"No, nobody touched him," Leverette said and moved out of room to let them get to work.

Chapter Twenty-Four

LEVERETTE SAT in his car trying to figure out just what the hell was going on. Why was his face hidden from Carole? Did this ever happen to her before? He made a mental note to ask her when he got to her house. This was a weird case.

He remembered working with a psychic on several cases and it worked out just fine.

Her name was Colleen, but he couldn't remember how to pronounce her last name. It was a rather long combination of consonants with a few vowels. Hungarian, he thought.

Colleen helped with the missing Bilsby boy. The nine-year-old went missing on his way home from a baseball game he'd played with the local kids.

His parents called and filed a report with the police, and like most parents, said he would never do anything like this. After interviewing his teachers and their pastor it seemed he'd have no reason to run away.

There was no ransom call, which the Bilsbys couldn't pay if one did come. Mr. Bilsby worked for a small company in Port Huron and Mrs. Bilsby was on disability. She was seriously injured in a car accident and was paralyzed from the waist down, not to mention she'd lost all function of her right arm because of a compound fracture that destroyed the nerves and tendons. In other words, they had no money.

Colleen had just moved into the area and worked for Customs at the Blue Water Bridge. She read about Bilsby in the paper and started getting feelings and came to talk to Billingsley. His first question was how much she wanted.

"I'm not here for money, Chief," she said. "I just want to help this young man. I just ask that my name be kept out of it."

He thanked her and agreed, still leery about why she didn't want money.

Billingsley believed in all this supernatural stuff, Leverette did a little, and asked her questions about what she could see.

"He's in an abandoned home," she said, "Very scared, not hurt. The woman has him chained to an old radiator, but he has enough length to get to the bathroom and his bedroom."

"Can you tell anything about the house or the neighborhood?"

"It looks like the block only has a few people living on it. The house is an old style two-story, white, several broken windows, front porch is caved in, black shingles, overgrown grass."

Billingsley finished writing everything down and asked, "Do you see street signs or anything that could help us find this house?"

Colleen thought for a minute. "No, sorry," she said.

"Would it help if you held something the boy owned?"

"Yes, it would," she said.

"I'll be right back," Billingsley said and got up to go to Leverette.

"You still have that shirt from the Bilsby case?"

"Sure," Leverette pulled his drawer open and handed it to the chief. "Why? What's up?"

"I'll let you know later, thanks," Billingsley said as he turned to go back to his office.

The evidence bag wasn't sealed since it was something his father brought from home. He took the tee shirt out and handed it to Colleen.

She held it in both hands and closed her eyes.

"He knows exactly where he is," Colleen said. "It's not an abandoned house just not kept up and in a rural area. That's why I thought it was an empty block." She closed her eyes again and tried to connect with Bilsby. Not that she could talk to him, just see his thoughts.

"The woman, Becky, is taking good care of him, like he's her son. He's not hungry, has new clothes, video games, but he wants to go home. She's getting upset every time he brings it up."

Again, she closed her eyes trying to peek into his mind. She balled the tee shirt up and squeezed it in her hands. Her eyes opened quickly.

"Something about a golf course," Colleen said, "Right across the street. Looks like they're building a new house in back of this one but it's quite some ways away. He's in a corner house."

Billingsley thought about the golf courses in the area. Only one in a rural area, Smith's Creek. Smith's Creek!

"Colleen, thank you for your help," he said and stood up. He was smiling and wanted to get Leverette and Saunders, who was Leverette's partner until he retired, and Marsden came aboard.

She looked at him and returned the smile, "Glad I could help." You didn't have to be psychic to know she solved had the case.

They found the boy right where Colleen said he would be.

Colleen didn't call or stop by the precinct after that for about five months. Another missing child.

Leverette wondered where she was now. He sure had some questions he needed answered. He wondered if Billingsley had Colleen's info.

As he got ready to pull into the drive, he saw Billingsley was already there. He wanted to go put his arms around Carole and tell her everything was going to be alright; she was going to be safe with him around. But not just to calm her, he longed to hold her, kiss her. He decided to go back to the precinct.

Michaels let Billingsley in this time. He noticed Carole and Amy sipping tea. He hated tea. His wife was always trying to get him to try chamomile to help him relax. After trying it the one time and gagging on it he decided bourbon would be better. He wasn't a drinker but if it was a case that wound him up, like this one, he did indulge.

The ladies were sitting where they were when he left. His officers were monitoring the house and he was proud of their dedication.

He sat in the chair that Leverette had been sitting in earlier and looked at Carole.

She saw the sadness in his eyes, and she started to cry. Amy put her arm around her to try to calm her down. It wasn't working.

"Ms. Sage, you did all you could," Billingsley started. "We found him, but he was already gone."

"I don't understand," Amy said, "Didn't you say the other man was killed three hours after Carole had her vision."

"Yes, he was," Billingsley said and sank back into the chair. "This was only an hour after, and we got there around 1:30 thinking we had time to set up to catch him."

Carole wiped her eyes with the last tissue in the box. Amy got up to throw it away and get a new one. She knew they'd be needing it.

"The owl," Carole said.

"What about it?" Billingsley asked.

"It only hooted once. With the young man it hooted three times."

"So..." Billingsley started to say, then understood what she was saying. "It let us know how long we had, and we didn't catch it."

"And why did he hide the face from me?"

"I don't know," Billingsley said, "You said you didn't know anyone on the list of witnesses."

Carol shook her head.

"Do you think he's psychic or something? That's why he hid the face?" Amy asked.

"I know someone I can call," Billingsley said. "She's a psychic and has helped us successfully with several cases. She may be able to help now, too."

He hoped Betty was still there, he didn't want to talk to Smith. Even though she was his nephew's wife. As a matter of fact, nobody wanted to ever talk to Smith.

He called Betty and breathed a sigh of relief when she said she was still there.

"I need to get something that belonged to Frank McCullough. Not anything you need for evidence, but maybe a shirt or something like that," Billingsley said.

"Sure, I'll drop it by the precinct when I'm on my way to the lab," she said and hung up.

Now if he could get a hold of Colleen things just might fall into place.

Chapter Twenty-Five

LEVERETTE STOPPED at the local twenty-four-hour diner to get breakfast and a good cup of coffee.

While waiting for his order he went over what he knew about the case so far. Not a damn thing! There's no way to find out who this creep is, no finger or footprints, no hair, not a fucking thing! Even the video of him was useless. He was wearing black with an open-faced stocking cap and large-framed sunglasses, all you could see were his nose and mouth.

When his order was ready, he paid for it and headed to his car. Just as he was going to slide in, Billingsley pulled up next to him.

"Great minds, right Joe?" Billingsley chuckled. "You going back to the precinct?"

"Yeah, I want to look over everything again," he said. "We must have missed something."

Billingsley nodded. "I'm going to call Colleen Hlavacek and see if she can help. Remember her?"

"Yeah, I was thinking about her too," Leverette said and smiled. "Great minds, Chief."

Billingsley nodded and headed into the restaurant; Leverette went to the precinct.

First thing Leverette did was to call Marsden and tell him what had happened.

"Sounds like the sting didn't work." Marsden said and yawned. "I'll be there as soon as I can."

"Okay. Billingsley will be here after he picks up some breakfast," Leverette said.

"Alright," Marsden said and hung up the phone. He'd pick up some doughnuts and coffee on his way in, he thought to himself. He was glad they didn't call him to the scene, he hated this case.

Betty walked into the precinct and went to Billingsley's office. The door was closed, and it was dark, so she looked toward the detective's desks and saw that Leverette was there.

She walked up to him, "Morning, Joe," she said and smiled at him.

He swallowed a mouthful of eggs and took a sip of coffee. "Hi," he said and wiped his mouth. "What brings you here?"

"I'm on my way to the lab and Billingsley asked me to drop this off," she said handing him an evidence bag with a tee shirt in it. "This isn't evidence."

"He'll be here soon. I'll give it to him," Leverette said and placed the bag on his desk. "Smith still there?"

"They were getting ready to put the body in the van when we left," she said. "I really can't stand that woman!"

"You and the rest of the precinct," Leverette said and they both chuckled.

"Well, I'm off to the lab to run the evidence we did get," she said and turned to leave.

"Yeah, have a good one," he said. She raised her right hand and gave him a backward wave.

Leverette finished his breakfast and threw the container and plastic silverware into the trash bin by his desk.

He turned on his computer to see if there were any new messages and he just about jumped out of his seat.

"The son of a bitch!" he said out loud just as Billingsley walked to his office door. He turned and noticed the look on Leverette's face and went to his desk.

"What is it, Joe?" he asked.

"That fucking bastard taped this one," Leverette said as he stared at the monitor. "Look!"

Billingsley came around the desk just as the murderer was putting the head in a black plastic trash bag.

"Holy shit!" Billingsley said and set his breakfast container on Leverette's desk. The two watched it all the way through.

The murderer held up a sheet of paper which had the message printed out in large letters.

'Five to go. The last will be your lady love. You'll never catch me.'.

"That last sentence is new," Billingsley said.

"And still with the count down," Leverette said. "He thinks we'll never catch him; he's wrong."

"Let's hope we do before he kills another person. I've a mind to warn the rest but I really don't want this to leak to the papers just yet," Billingsley said. "It's probably what he wants."

"I don't think so," Leverette said. "I have a gut feeling he's just playing with us and doesn't care about publicity. I'll get this down to Andy."

"Good, let me know if he can find anything out."

"Yeah, he should be in around seven."

"I'm going to call Colleen now. Betty's supposed to drop off something that belonged to Frank for me."

"Oh, she already did," Leverette said and handed him the evidence bag. "She said it wasn't evidence."

"Great, I wanted this for Colleen. Personal items help her," Billingsley said and took the package from Leverette and picked up his breakfast. "I'll be in my office if you need me."

Leverette decided to save it before he sent it to Andy. As he pressed the save button the video went dark and a hand appeared with its middle finger extended and a message 'Fuck you, Joseph Leverette you'll never catch me' then the screen went dark. He went back to the e-mail, but the video was gone.

"Damn it!" he said out loud. He'd have to wait until

Andy got in to tell him what happened. Maybe he'd know how to get it back.

Marsden walked in just as Leverette yelled. He went and put the box of doughnuts by the coffee machine, picked one out for himself then headed to their desks.

"What's up?" he asked.

"That bastard sent a video to my e-mail address," Leverette said, "I don't know how he got it."

"What's the video about?"

"It was his last murder. From beginning to end. With another message at the end."

"You're not going to make me watch it, are you?" Marsden said wide eyed.

"You don't have to worry about that," Leverette said and sat back in his chair. "The bastard fixed it so it would delete if I tried to save it. Probably would have deleted if I forwarded it."

Marsden was grateful, in a way, but he knew the video might help with the investigation.

"Maybe Andy can figure something out," Marsden said and went to his side of the desk. He took off his coat and hooked it on the back of his chair. Just as he was going to sit down Billingsley called them to come into his office.

Chapter Twenty-Six

THE TWO DETECTIVES went into the office holding their coffee's in their hands and took their seats.

"I spoke to Colleen just now and she'll stop in in about an hour, Billingsley said.

Leverette nodded and Marsden was a bit confused.

"Is that the lady who helped in the past?" Marsden asked, "I heard stories about someone when I first came on."

"Yes, she's been a great help. I'm hoping she'll be able to help us now," Billingsley said. "She might even be able to work with Ms. Sage to understand what kind of visions she was having."

"What time does Andy come in?" Billingsley asked.

"He should be here at seven. I'll talk to him before I send the email just in case the asshole put something else in it and it fucks up our whole system," Leverette said and took a sip of his coffee.

"Okay, that's in about ten minutes. Let me know what he finds, immediately."

"Sure thing, Chief," Leverette said, then he and Marsden headed back to their desks.

Amy took the day off; fortunately, her boss was understanding about what was going on with her friend, Carole.

Carole had fallen asleep on the couch and was still there when Amy came down. Instead of waking her she went into the kitchen and put a pot of coffee on.

Carole stirred as the aroma of the coffee filled the air. She sat up and looked into the kitchen where Amy was getting things ready to make breakfast.

Amy caught sight of her from the corner of her eye. "Good morning, sleepy head," she said and smiled. "How are you feeling?"

"Okay, I guess," Carole said and stretched before she got up and headed to the kitchen. "What's on the menu?"

"How about a farmer's omelet?" Amy asked as she pulled the eggs and vegetables out of the fridge.

"Sounds good," Carole said and stretched again. She winced this time as she felt a pinch in her back. "I'll go get dressed."

"Okay, it'll be ready when you come down."

Carole headed upstairs, took a quick shower and dressed.

Amy was buttering the four slices of toast when Carole came back into the kitchen. She went and poured herself a cup of coffee.

They sat down and started eating. Carole was surprised she was so hungry. She'd had dinner last night and this was so unusual for her.

"You must really be hungry," Amy said and smiled at her friend. "I've never seen you eat so fast. You better slow down."

"I'm surprised, too," Carole chuckled. "Must be stress from all this shit."

"Could very well be," Amy agreed.

Bud was out in the back yard and started barking. The two friends looked at each other, both feeling a cold chill going down their backs.

Amy stood up and slowly walked to the back door. Carole went to a cabinet in the kitchen and got her gun. She'd had it since she graduated, by her father's insistence. He didn't like his little girl going out on her own with no protection.

Carole's backyard was fenced in with a four-foot-tall chain link fence, but Amy knew Bud could clear it in one jump. He did meet the officers and detectives last night and seemed to like them all.

His barks turned more vicious, scaring the ladies even more. Carole walked to the back door, gun at the ready, and opened the door.

Nobody was there, but Bud was still upset. Amy

called for him to come in the house. He hesitated, looking to the front of the house, but obeyed her.

Once inside, he immediately ran to the front door and started sniffing and growling. He wasn't happy with something.

Carole moved to the long window on the left side of the door and looked out. She didn't see anyone but there was a small, flat box on the front step.

"Someone left a box," she said to Amy.

"Did you order anything?" Amy was still shaking.

"No," was all Carole said. "I think I'll call Billingsley and let him know."

"Good idea," Amy said moving to the window on the other side of the door and looked out. "You don't know what it could be."

Carole set the safety on her gun and put it back in the cabinet. She went into the living room and picked up her cell phone and dialed.

"Billingsley," he sounded upset.

"Chief, this is Carole Sage. Someone left a package on my front step just now."

"Did you open it?"

"No, it's still outside."

"Okay, I'll send Leverette and Marsden right over," he said and hung up.

She set her phone down and told Amy what he had said.

"Good. I wonder what's in it?" Amy wondered out loud.

"I don't know," Carole said. "Let's finish breakfast."

They went back to the kitchen, freshened up their coffee and sat back at the table. Both were still shaking and had lost their appetites. They sipped their coffee and sat in silence.

Then Bud, who had finally decided to lie down, sat up and listened looking toward the front door. He started wagging his tail.

"Well, that's a good sign," Amy said and reached down to scratch his head.

"Good boy," she told him. He looked up at her and ran for the front door just as someone knocked.

Carole looked at Amy then got up to see who was there. She was relieved when she saw it was Leverette.

Opening the door made Bud go crazy. Jumping and whining wanting him to come in. Carole unlocked the outer door and let him in.

"This is the package?" he asked looking down at it. He noticed it was the same handwriting as the one with the King's boys head and he was pretty sure the return address was, too. When they had checked it out, they found it was an empty lot.

"Yeah, it was left here a few minutes ago," Carole said as he came into her home. "The chief said not to touch it until he and some others come here. We had no intention of touching it anyway."

Bud jumped on Leverette and he was absent mindedly rubbing behind his ears. He loved dogs, all animals really, and they seemed to love him.

"Bud, get down," Amy called from the kitchen. Bud turned to look at her and eventually got down and reluctantly went over to her.

"Would you like some coffee, Detective?" Amy called from the kitchen.

"Sure, and you both can call me Joe when the chief's not around."

He followed Carole into the kitchen and waited for the two ladies to sit, then sat himself. Amy handed him his coffee.

He took a sip then turned to Carole, "Did you see a vehicle or a person?"

"No, we had no idea anything was going on until Bud went ape-shit," she said. "When we did look outside, we didn't see anything."

Leverette nodded, wondering if the guy was still nearby. He couldn't have gotten far if he was on foot, but if he had a car parked close, he could very well be gone.

Amy looked at Leverette; she was terrified again.

Do you think he'll come here?" she asked.

"No, I don't think so," was all Leverette decided to say. He didn't want to scare them any more than they already were. They had no idea in what order this maniac was going but he did know Carole would be the last. He had no intention of it getting even close to that.

Leverette decided to change the subject, so he asked Amy about Bud to fill in the time until Billingsley got there.

The knock on the door made the ladies jump and Bud

took notice but didn't bark. They heard voices just outside and Leverette went to answer the door.

"Leverette, why am I not surprised?" Billingsley said not really wanting an answer. "Did you see anything on your way over?"

"Hi Chief," Leverette's cheeks started to blush. "Nobody was around, and I got here pretty quick."

"Betty and her team are out there now, looking things over," Billingsley said. He went past Leverette to talk to the two women who stood looking scared.

"Good morning, ladies," Billingsley said to them.

"We just put a fresh pot of coffee on, Chief, would you like a cup?" Carole said and walked up to the coffee maker.

"Thank you, that would be great," he said and sat down at the table. Bud came over and nudged him. Billingsley reached down and scratched him behind the ears.

Carole put his coffee in front of him and sat down.

"Did either of you see or hear anything unusual before you found the box?"

"No," they answered almost in unison.

"Bud was outside and started to go crazy, so we brought him in," Carole told him. "He went straight to the front door after we let him in and that's when we saw that box."

Leverette nodded and thought, *this is a fucked-up case. First this guy hacks up this woman and spreads her parts all over the area, then goes after the people who found the parts. And they have a sensitive who actually visualized the murder. Shit, this is one for the books.*

He decided to change the conversation and looked at Bud.

"He's a good watch dog," he said to them.

"Yes, he's been trained," Amy said. Their conversation, from that point on, focused on Bud.

A knock on the door made the women jump but Bud just sat there wagging his tail. Leverette got up, put his hand on his gun and walked to the door. He looked through the pigeonhole and relaxed.

"It's okay ladies," he said, "It's Billingsley and the team."

"Morning, Chief," Leverette said opening the door for him and the team to enter. Betty and another of her team stayed outside and started looking around.

"'Morning Ladies," he said.

"Morning Chief," Carole said. Amy smiled and nodded. "Would you like some coffee? I just made it."

"Thanks, that would be great. It's so damn cold out there! Is this winter ever going to end?" he said and sat at the table by Carole.

Leverette picked up his coffee and stood beside Billingsley.

As Carole was getting the coffee, the other investigator, Brenda, asked Amy to tell her what happened.

Amy went through what had happened and showed her the back door. Brenda had her gloves on already, so she opened it and went out to look around the yard.

Betty knocked on the door then came in.

"There's nothing electrical in it," she said to Billingsley. The she turned to Carole and Amy. "Would it be all right if we brought it in here to open? It's so damn cold out there."

"Sure," Carole said even though she didn't want to see what was in it.

"Thanks," Betty said and went back out front and a few seconds later she and Tom came in. She put a cloth on the table and then set the box on it.

The box was wrapped in a white paper that was treated on the one side. Tom had evidence bags ready.

She took the wrapper off and placed it in one of the large bags. The box was also white and looked like something you'd put jewelry in. It was six inches square and maybe one inch deep.

Betty opened the box and saw that it held a piece of paper. She carefully removed the paper and put it on the cloth she'd put down earlier, then put the box in another bag.

Carole and Amy hovered and wanted to see what was on the note. Well, Carole wasn't sure she wanted to, but she looked anyway.

Betty, who had no trouble keeping a straight face, read it, and handed it to Billingsley. He pulled a glove out his pocket and, instead of putting it on, used it to hold a corner of the note. He tried not to react but is shocked by what it had written on it.

"What is it, Chief?" Carole asked. She was starting to

shake and to look ashen. He didn't know if he should read it to her or hand it to her. Billingsley did know that he wanted her to sit down before she fainted.

"Why don't you sit there and I'll read it to you?" He said. Carole was shaking so hard at this point that Amy had to help her.

Billingsley cleared his throat and read:

"I know who you are

And what you see.

But neither you or the cops

Will ever catch me!"

Tears start streaming down Carole's face and she clasped her hands over her mouth so she wouldn't scream. Leverette wanted badly to go and hold her but knew he couldn't. It was breaking his heart to see her like this.

Billingsley was beside himself. He hated when women cried and felt especially bad for Carole. What she must be going through!

"We can move you to a safe house, both of you and Bud," Billingsley said hoping the tears in his eyes weren't too visible.

Betty and her team finished and said goodbye to everyone. They wanted to get this to the lab and start on it immediately. Plus, Betty knew the chief wanted to talk privately to the women.

As they left, Marsden had just walked up to the door shivering from the cold.

He walked into the kitchen with his arms folded across his chest.

"Morning," he said. Everyone responded and Amy got up to pour him a cup of coffee. He pulled his gloves off and wrapped his fingers around it letting them warm up.

"Thank you ever so much!" he said and looked at fear-stricken Carole.

Before he could ask, Billingsley told him about the note.

He let out a long whistle. "Are we going to move them to a safe house?"

Carole was in no shape to answer so Amy said, "I think that would be a good idea."

Billingsley looked at Carole who seemed like she was almost catatonic.

"Ms. Sage?"

She looked up and nodded so he took that as a yes.

"Why don't they just stay at my place, Chief?" Marsden asked. "I have a fenced in yard for the dog. My neighbors aren't that close to my house so there'll be some privacy."

Billingsley, without waiting for Leverette to answer, spoke right away. "What do you ladies think?"

"Is that something that's done?" Amy asked.

"Yes, it is," Billingsley answered. "And I don't think we have anyplace else that would accommodate Bud."

Amy put her had on Carole's shoulder causing her to shudder. Carole just nodded her head and Amy wondered if she even heard anything that was being said.

Leverette knew it wouldn't work at his place; even though he had a large back yard it wasn't completely fenced in, and that would be a problem. He did feel safe about them staying with Marsden, though.

"We don't know if he's watching so we'll have to do this as carefully as we can."

He pulled out his cell phone and pressed the speed dial key.

"Paul, I need your help again."

Chapter Twenty-Seven

THEY ARRANGED for the women to meet them at a restaurant. The same one Billingsley and Leverette had gone to for breakfast. The owners were told about the two female officers who were going to be there shortly to take the women's' places.

Carole and Amy arrived and parked in the back like they were told. Marsden was already there so they loaded their suitcases in the trunk and put Bud in the backseat. They weren't going to be but a couple of minutes and there was a blanket for him to curl up in.

Hanz, the owner, was waiting by the back door and let them in. He was excited about being part of this 'operation' and was sworn to secrecy. His wife, Trudy, took a little more convincing but finally agreed. He led them to a back room for the meeting.

Billingsley and Leverette were already waiting for them inside.

"Okay, this is what happens from here," Billingsley said. "You two are going with Marsden, and Leverette will follow closely behind," he stopped to be sure the women were understanding him. He hadn't wanted to tell them too much about his plan until now.

"Will our cars be safe here?" Amy asked.

"They're not going to stay here," Billingsley told them. Just then two women walked in through the back door. Again, Hanz was smiling at his part in this.

"Ah, they're here," Billingsley said, "These two officers are going to be taking your place so please give them your house and car keys. We'll also need you both to exchange your coats, hats, gloves, and purses. This is Mary Angelique and Sue Harker. They're close to your sizes and should fool him."

"I'm not going to be thinking too much about what we're doing just in case he is a sensitive himself," Carole said.

Mary looked confused. "You mean a sensitive can read minds?" she asked.

"No but we can see spirits, or what they want us to see," Carole said. "Somehow I think he's tricking them so he can find me."

"Do you think this will fool him? After all you're not going back to the house, we are."

"I'm planning on thinking that I'm back at the house instead of going to the detective's house. That should help."

Mary looked at Billingsley, wanting confirmation that this would work. He nodded and she was satisfied.

"Okay, let's get going," Billingsley said and Hanz led the two officers to the back door, watching that they got to the cars safely. Satisfied he went back to the others.

Once they pulled away, the women followed Marsden out to his car. Bud sat up when he heard them coming toward the car.

"Now I know it'll be a bit uncomfortable, but the two of you need to squeeze in back with Bud and keep down until I pull into my garage."

They both nodded and got Bud to lie on the floor of the car. Then they stretched out on the seat and lay next to each other.

Marsden saw they were all situated and started the car, then pulled out heading toward his home.

Carole had pictured driving to her house the whole time, as if she were driving her car, hoping like hell that this was going to fool him.

"Okay, Joe, you head over to Carole's like you always do," Billingsley said to Leverette.

Leverette started to say something, but Billingsley held up his hand.

"I know you've been there every night and that's not here nor there. He probably knows you were, or has seen you, there. We don't want anything to change in that respect."

"Okay, Chief," Leverette said, glad he wasn't going to get a reprimand. "I'll head right over."

"Good, let me know if anything happens," Billingsley said and headed outside with his order for dinner.

Leverette grabbed his own order and a cup of coffee and followed right behind.

The ride to Marsden's was a little bumpy and he tried his best not to jostle his precious cargo. He heard a couple groans coming from the back and felt bad.

He pulled into his drive and opened the garage door with his remote then pulled in. Once the door was closed completely, he breathed a sigh of relief.

"Okay, ladies, we're here," he said as he opened his door. He opened the back door on his side and helped Amy up first, then Carole. Bud jumped out the minute it was clear. Amy took out the blanket Bud was lying on and shut the door. She set Oscar's cat carrier on the floor and opened it to let him out.

They walked to the back of the car and got their suitcases out while Marsden took Bud out the back door to his business.

He unlocked the door to the house and the three went in. He would let Bud in thought the French doors off the kitchen.

"Okay, I have two bedrooms down the hall and an extra bathroom," he said and motioned down the hall. "I'm down here on the other end."

"We'll get freshened up and put our things away," Amy said. Carole was trying hard not to think about where they were. At times she wished the spirits would help her.

Marsden was starving. Unlike Billingsley and Leverette, he hadn't thought to order dinner for him or his house guests. It wouldn't be safe to go out for take-out, but it was still early enough to get a pizza delivered.

"Ladies, I'm about to order pizza for dinner. Any requests?"

They both walked into the dining room and said no. Amy walked over to the French doors and let Bud in.

"Where can I set up his food and water dishes?"

Put them closer to the inside of the kitchen. That way he won't be as visible to prying eyes."

Amy set him up and walked back into the dining room. She was impressed with how neat Marsden was, you'd never guess he was a bachelor. She remembered going to her brother's house and seeing the mess. Clothes everywhere, dirty dishes, empty pizza boxes, she smiled to herself remembering.

She saw Marsden look at her. "You have a beautiful home," she said hoping he wasn't going to ask what she was smiling about.

"Thank you," he said. "I'll order the pizza. It usually

takes about twenty minutes. I have beer if either of you want one. Or I could put coffee on."

"Beer sounds about right," Carole said. "That's what I'm having at home right now."

The three chuckled as Marsden went to get the beers from the fridge. Once he got back to the table Carole started the conversation.

"I think I want to paint this year," she started. They all knew she wanted to have her house in her mind.

"I'm thinking of doing a soft peach on the walls and trim with a pale turquoise."

"That sounds pretty," Amy said. "And your living room furniture will match so well."

"Yes, they'll set it off just right," Carole said. "I saw some drapes that would be perfect, too."

Marsden decided not to join in the conversation and sat at the farthest part of the table. He figured that would be a distraction for Carole, so he just enjoyed the women's company.

They continued on about curtains, throw rugs and such until the pizza came. Marsden went to the door and got the pizza.

Amy shushed Bud when he started growling in his throat. She figured this was all new to him.

"Eating kinda late?" the delivery man asked.

"Had a busy day," was all Marsden said to him. He gave him a tip and closed the door.

Amy noticed a concerned look on his face and went into the kitchen to help him with plates and napkins.

"What's wrong?"

"He was new," Marsden said.

"Maybe he just started working for them," she said.

"It's a family-owned pizzeria and very authentic. Only family works for them. I don't know him."

A scream echoed from the dining room.

Marsden and Amy quickly ran into the dining room to see what was wrong.

Before they could ask, Carole looked at Marsden.

"Did he ask you 'Eating kinda late?'?" she asked Marsden.

Marsden sat down next to her and in a low voice said, "Yes".

"He knows I'm here! That was him!" Carole was frantic.

Amy, who was on the other side of her, put her arm around her shoulders.

Marsden pulled his cell from his pocket and called Billingsley.

"Fuck! How the hell did he know?" Billingsley was pissed.

"I have no idea, Chief. Carole knew it was him, though."

"Call Leverette and have him stay with you tonight just in case he shows up again."

"Okay Chief," Marsden said and hung up then called Leverette and told him what was going on. He said he'd be there as soon as possible. Marsden told the women what was happening, but this didn't do much to calm Carole down. She was scared hysterical.

Marsden, who was used to this kind of stress, sat down and ate a piece of pizza. He was starving.

Amy and Carole were each nibbling on the slice they each took. They were hungry but just couldn't bring themselves to eat.

Leverette arrived twenty-five minutes after the call and pulled into the driveway. He drew his gun and walked around the house to be sure it was clear. When he got to the back of the house he almost jumped out of his skin when Bud barked at him from the kitchen through the French doors. He continued around to the front of the house then, seeing that nobody was around, went to knock on the door.

Marsden was already there and opened it just before he knocked, making him jump.

"Getting jumpy in your old age?" Marsden teased.

Leverette just glared at him, making Marsden chuckle.

After Leverette was in the house Marsden locked the outside and inside doors.

"They're in the dining room. There's some pizza if you're hungry."

"Thanks," was all Leverette said. When he walked into the dining room, he saw Carole with tears streaming down her face and Amy trying to console her. How he ached to have her in his arms telling her she'll be safe with him.

He sat next to Carole and looked up at Amy.

"Does she have something to take the edge off?" he asked, "besides the beer?"

"Yes, but she doesn't like to take it. It puts her totally out, even if she takes half a pill."

Marsden had gone through the house checking that the windows are locked, which he knew they were, but this case was weird, and he had to check them. The garage door to the house was locked, the French doors were locked. They should be all right.

"Well, we should take shifts through the night," Marsden said to Leverette as he walked back into the dining room.

"I don't know if I can sleep," Amy said.

"Knowing Billingsley, he'll have a patrol car in the area. It'll be all right," Marsden said knowing they'd be safe because the killer said Carole was going to be his last murder.

Carole wiped her eyes with her napkin and finished her beer. She was trying so hard to calm herself down. Marsden noticed she was done and offered her another beer, hoping it would help her sleep.

"If it's no trouble," she said in almost a whisper.

"No problem. Ms. Lang would you like another?"

"Sure," she said. She was so worried about her friend.

Carole didn't tell her about the note he left at the first murder about her being the last. Amy was probably going to be the one he killed just before her.

Leverette turned the beer down because he wanted to

be alert for the night. One beer, especially with him so wound up, would make him sleepy.

When Carole and Amy finished their beers, they decided to go to sleep.

"We'll be in the bedroom on the right," Amy said. "Neither of us wants to be alone tonight especially now."

"Okay," Marsden said. "Good night. One of us will be awake throughout the night."

"Good night," Amy said. Carole just nodded and let Amy lead her to the bedroom.

"I'll take first watch," Leverette said. "I'm pretty wired."

"Okay, my room is down this way," Marsden pointed to the other side of the house. "You already know where the bathroom is."

"I'll get you up in four hours," Leverette told him. This was always the best length of time for this kind of situation.

"Good night," Marsden said and headed to bed.

Leverette sat at the dining room table. He knew if he sat in the chair or sofa in the living room, he'd fall asleep.

Bud lay down at his feet instead of staying with the women. It was as if he wanted to help protect them.

Time was passing relatively fast which made Leverette nervous. This always dragged on and on but not now.

He'd get up and look out the windows then sit back down. He wondered what this fucker was up to.

Carole was dreaming, maybe, she couldn't tell when

she was asleep until she woke up. In the dream a man driving a car was laughing hysterically. His face was in shadow, so she didn't know who he was.

A semi's horn blared, followed by a thunderous crashing. Then the single hoot of an owl, woke Carole from her sleep.

She sat straight up in bed scaring Amy.

"What's wrong?" Amy asked trying to stifle a yawn.

"He's dead!"

"Who?"

"The murderer!" Carol said and got up running the dining room. Amy was quick on her heels.

Leverette had just sat down from checking outside. He heard the footsteps and jumped up.

"He's dead!" she said with the first real smile Leverette had seen on her face.

Marsden heard the commotion and put his robe on, heading down the hall.

"What happened?" he said, his adrenalin flowing and fully awake.

"She said the murderer is dead," Leverette said.

"Yes, I saw him die. It was a horrible vehicle accident. He's dead!"

To be continued …

About the Author

Viv Drewa's work celebrates the spirit of the adventuresome woman. She is a Michigan native who has enjoyed reading and writing since 1963.

Though she studied medicinal chemistry at the University of Michigan her passion has always been writing. She spends her free time working with physically and mentally challenged adults; a cause close to her heart. She and her husband, Bob, live in Fort Gratiot, Michigan with their cat, Princess.

Also by VIV DREWA

Please check out my other titles here:

https://www.lavishpublishing.com/authors/viv-drewa/

Also from the Lavish Publishing family

The Norn Novellas

A. Nicky Hjort

https://www.lavishpublishing.com/authors/nicky-hjort-1/

The Norn Novellas are all chapters in the epic saga of the youngest and most fickle of the four Norn Sisters. The same feisty immortal creature who must escape her inherent inner darkness to learn the meaning of life.

Each story takes a classic fairytale and spins it on its head, as we learn that maybe Norse Mythology was so much more than legend. And to think, you thought you knew those old tales so well.

Meet Za and find out what really happened...

Teach me to Prey

Samantha Jacobey

https://www.lavishpublishing.com/authors/samantha-jacobey/

Taboo love stories give you a special thrill?

Rebecca Stewart had never let things get personal with her students; a mistake that could cost her far more than a broken heart.

Jason and his friends enjoyed tormenting teachers. When they set their sights on Miss Stewart, nothing would prevent them from bringing her down.

Avoiding Jason's advances and navigating an epic clash of wills, the young woman felt relieved to see graduation day finally arrive. Little did she know, it wouldn't end there. Pregnant and alone, she could only keep her secrets for so long.

After one of the boys is found murdered, the police haul her in, but she denies having done anything wrong. Can she convince them of the truth before all three of the young men fall victim to a killer, forcing her to raise her child alone?

Between the Trees

Kathy Moczerniak

https://www.lavishpublishing.com/authors/kathy-moczerniak/

A beautiful coming of age with a dark side that one teenager must fight to overcome...

Beyond Kathryn Lucas' first memory of her father's tree lay a dysfunctional path of violence, heartbreak, and secrets within a family severely entrenched in the vicious cycle of abuse. A lifetime of fear drives her from her home, and the teenage girl finds refuge with an aunt and uncle determined to protect their niece.

Distressing flashbacks unravel in Kathryn's fragile mind among the turmoil encircling her as she struggles through adolescence and descends into her pain-ridden past. When the summation of her unsettling memories allows the darkness to overtake her, she becomes desperate to unearth the light.

Inspired by a true story, Kathryn must hold on tightly to those who love her, searching for her place in a world threatening to break her as she fights to overcome life's betrayals before she is deprived of her future.